To
Th

Bob H

It's A
Long, Long
Line

A glimpse into eternity

Bob Highlands III

It's A Long, Long Line
a glimpse into eternity

ISBN: 9781794202719
Independently published

BobHighlands.com for more information

DEDICATED

To members of my church

Who look to me

to tell them the truth.

Contents

FORWARD ix

PROLOGUE 13

THE LAST DAY 15

AN APPOINTMENT TO KEEP 15

CROSSING OVER 29

FIRST CONTACT 45

THE TRIUMPHAL ENTRY 62

THE FRONT OF THE LINE 68

THE VIEWING PLATFORM 85

THE JUSTICE SEAT OF GOD SISTER ETHEL 96

THE LONG LONG LINES 108

SUDDENLY 112

A SECOND CHANCE 114

EPILOGUE A PERSONAL CHOICE TO MAKE 125

ABOUT THE AUTHOR 134

END NOTES 136

Bob Highlands III

FORWARD

What if everything we thought we knew about dying was not true? I was on vacation in a small Oregon coastal town. My wife and I were going from store to store when we stopped into one of those small bookstores you find in every coastal town. They all seem to have the most eclectic collection of books for sale. I can browse for hours reading passages from books I would never read otherwise. I often buy several to read later. You can never have too many books, and I guarantee I don't have too many, but I have plenty to read. As I walked around this one, I thought of all the different types of books and marveled at the subjects they covered. Then I asked myself a question, what was missing. What viewpoint had not been included? It came to me in a flash. What was it like to die and discover you were wrong and completely out of the will of God? C. S. Lewis came close to this in one of my favorite books 'The Great Divorce.[1]' Lewis places his hero on a flying transport taking people from the darkness to the light and along the way shows the life we live here before we die directly determines where we will spend eternity. People want to blame God or make excuses, but all He (God) does is honor the choices we make before we die.

There are plenty of books talking about some average person who dies and gets to go to heaven where they receive a special message from God. They come back with a picture of heaven that does not in the slightest resemble the heaven of scriptures. The message these heavenly travelers bring back with them almost always contradicts the message spoken by the Son of God when He was here with us and sounds more like wishful thinking than anything God would say. Before you send me a letter or email explaining how your experience is different, please consider the simple question I ask anyone who has had such an experience. Does this line up with the teachings found in the Word of God? Do you think people get to die and skip the judgment and then find themselves roaming around in heaven having lived a sinful life? Then they get to come back to earth from heaven with a watered-down message that comes down to 'go and be good?' This in contrast to what Jesus said to the woman in the New Testament, "Go now and leave your life of sin." Please consider the message of this book before it is you who is facing the living God. It is based on a simple understanding of death, the resurrection and eternal judgment put forth by Jesus in the New Testament.

I have never been to heaven and seriously doubt any of the people who claim to have been there having had anything beyond some near-death dream experience that would soothe their conscience. I have decided to use allegory to describe and convey the essence of what it would be like to die and face the question of what happens to the soul after the person passes from this life to the next. I base this book not on some personal experience after a near-death accident but what we do know from the Bible. There is a wealth of material that shows us the truth, and which debunks most books written about heaven and angels.

The image of judgment for this book comes not from my imagination but an old gospel song written by

Reba Rambo and Kenny Parker. Their song from 1970 titled "It's a Long, Long Line"[2] tells the story of people after they have died and find themselves waiting in line with others who have died and are to be judged by God. By the end of this book, you may well agree why I think they got it right and we all will stand in those long, long lines.

Finally, I believe with all my being that the Word of God is the inspired voice of God filled with truth and guidance. You can ignore it, deny it or fight against it but you will not outlive it.

Regrets will be the least of the worries for those who pay no attention to it. I submit the following for your consideration.

Bob Highlands III

PROLOGUE

The fool has said in his heart,
"There is no God." ^{Psalm 14.1}

The world is full of people preparing. We start preparing early and must do it the rest of our natural lives. Grade school prepares us for middle school. Middle school prepares us for high school, high school for college, college for a job. All the while we are preparing to take a vacation or working on a plan to lose weight so we can look good at the next class reunion or be able to fit into a new swimsuit for that vacation. People spend their life preparing for retirement by putting money into IRA accounts while trying to make all the other ends meet. All the preparing is so we can live a comfortable life until we die. But how many people prepare for what happens after they die?

Life is full of all types of people living day to day without ever considering eternity. Many of them are not like the fool who says, "There is no God." They believe there is a God but live their life with an attitude that there is no way to prepare, so they ignore what comes after death. Out of sight and out of mind is their motto for eternity. Some soothe their need for God in their life with synthetic manmade religions. They believe they can earn their way to heaven or that a God of love will let them into eternity with Him because… Well, most of them have never contemplated that thought.

What if there is a God? What if He has guidelines for who gets in and who does not? What if you are not ready when the end comes? What happens then? What is it like to die and pass from this life to the next? What if your life was about to be measured in minutes and seconds? What would you do differently?

THE LAST DAY

And I'll say to myself, "You have plenty of good
things laid up for many years. Take life easy;
eat, drink and be merry."'
"But God said to him, 'You fool! This very night
your life will be demanded from you. Then who
will get what you have prepared for yourself?
Luke 12.19-20

Winston James Cummings had just five minutes and
thirty-four seconds to live as he stepped out of his
office and pulled the door shut behind him.

This day had gone the same as thousands of others that
had proceeded it. Up first in the house, he had
showered, shaved and been able to use the bathroom
before anyone else was up. He had gone through
thirty-five emails and two sports websites in the quiet
of the bathroom when suddenly he heard yelling and
knew the girls were up. Breakfast had been chaos with
the two girls arguing about some silly computer game
everyone was playing at school. His wife, Sarah, was
running late for her job and needed his help getting the
girls motivated. Why she had asked him for help was
beyond him. They never listened to him. The little
princesses had learned early in their lives that dad was
all bark and no bite, so they were now utterly oblivious
to anything he told them to do. The only way he got
them to listen was with bribes, and they were now

15

holding out for more before doing what he wanted. It was getting expensive for him to have any leverage over them at all. Kissing his wife on the cheek to not smear her lipstick and patting the girls on the head as he went by was all he intended. Then, Mavin the youngest, who was named after her mother's sister's favorite singer, ran after him.

"Hey, you." She said with a stern voice. "Where are my kiss and hug?" She was in the hall with her arms out and her cutest expression of 'ain't I sweet' on her face, ever. This face led to a hug for everyone and kisses all around, even his wife, and a dash to the car. Winston had about ten hours and fifty-three minutes to live.

He pulled into the park and ride as the bus was coming down the ramp from the freeway, so he had to dash across the parking lot. The bus driver was a sixty-four-year-old woman who he had mistaken for a man on his first day he rode the bus, and she had never forgiven him. She had now been on this route for five years, and every day started with a stare that said, 'Go ahead, open your mouth and I will chew your head off.' He boarded and moved toward the middle of the bus. He had read that in an accident, people in the middle of the bus are less likely to die or be as seriously injured. He did not know if it was true, but he was not going to take any chances. On the ride to work, he had clocked in over the server using the link on his phone and started working on his computer. About half of the trip he would be on a sports page catching up on the morning reports for his fantasy league but would charge it to his office hours.

The ride averaged one hour and thirty-eight minutes. It was only 45 miles to the transfer station, but the traffic was horrendous and getting worse every year. Last year the regional traffic commission had finished a traffic revision at the cost of four hundred and sixty-five million dollars that had looked great on paper five years ago but with the flood of new workers, had in effect, only made things worse. It used to take one hour but with the new lane restrictions, tolls and increased traffic he might soon have to sleep at the office during the week. The traffic commission had come up with a new plan to double the number of bus riders in the area from 2 percent to 4 percent in 10 years at the cost of 5 billion dollars. It had been approved in the general election last year but looked like it was about to be pulled. When people started getting their car tab bills at four times what they used to be and double property taxes to cover it, the revolt had begun. He arrived at the transfer station, and he could see his bus downtown pulling out. He would have to wait for another 12 minutes for the next bus. Winston had eight hours and forty-two minutes to live.

It had been raining when he arrived at the transfer station. It seemed strange to outsiders that no one in the area, where it rains half the year, uses an umbrella.

He had grown up here and was not going to be the only one using an umbrella and thus be weird. He darted to the platform in the steady rain like mist and hugged up against the building to wait for his bus downtown. Late, as usual, the bus arrived after nineteen minutes and was packed to overflowing. The combination of commuters trying to get to work and the homeless trying to get out of the rain by using the free bus passes given out by a local homeless advocacy group the bus was an angry, smelly ride every time it was raining. He stood, refusing to sit on the stained seats. At his stop, he had to force his way out, and a woman with purple hair on one side of her head and the other side shaved Marine Corps close screamed obscenities at him for tripping over her backpack that she had put down in the center of the aisle of the bus. As he opened the door to his office, he had seven hours and fifty-four minutes to live.

The morning had been filled with phone calls, text messages, a brief meeting to discuss the retirement of one of the secretaries who he was glad to see leave and listening to his favorite sports radio through his new almost invisible mini earplug while he surfed news and sports websites. He was looking forward to lunch and spending time with Donna. She was his previous secretary who had a job across town at another firm. For a while, they had been very close. Though they had never crossed the line physically, they always seemed to be as close to an intimate relationship as two people could have without physical contact. They had agreed to be friends when she left and had never done anything physically inappropriate but shared lunch and an occasional dinner. She was ten years younger than him and unmarried. She was buying him lunch to celebrate his most recent promotion. It would be a long lunch as it always was with Donna. He always enjoyed his time with her and thought that if he had met her first his world would be very different.

More than once he had found himself daydreaming about spending his life with her or having a more intimate relationship. The lunch was a highlight of his week, and they had talked and laughed for several hours. Winston was surprised and flattered when at the end of lunch, she hugged him to congratulate him for his promotion and then kissed him on the cheek before walking away. She stopped at the corner and looked back as she smiled at him and he could not hold it in and smiled back. Things were changing, and he liked the feeling of excitement and adventure it brought to him. Maybe dreams do come true. Winston was less than three hours and twenty-four minutes away from a very tragic accident and an appointment with death.

The walk back to his office took ten minutes. As he walked, he was in a daydream about spending time with Donna on a more intimate level. He sat down at his desk and clicked on his computer monitor. There was his favorite picture of his wife, the girls and him that was taken at the beach last summer. He smiled and went back to work.

He had spent the last fifteen years happily married. His wife was a committed believer, and she and the girls were in church every Sunday. Winston, on the other hand, kept it down to the necessary family events he could not avoid without causing world war three at his house. There was the Christmas pageant, Easter, the summer carnival and usually right after school started to get things back on track after the summer. It never worked. He went and was able to tune out the message while he arranged his dream fantasy sports team in his head. All that guilt stuff was not for him. God, if there was a God, was not going to eat up his precious little time. He made sure something was happening on Sunday mornings. Anything was better than going to church. Last Saturday he had taken the family to the local farmers market for a community festival honoring the different species that share this planet. There were all sorts of religions represented, and they all seemed to want to get along. The coexist stickers made in the shape of all the major faiths were everywhere, and he had bought one for the minivan which had not made his wife happy. That was his idea of religion and the full amount of his relationship with God, whoever he or she was.

His best friend Mark called and wanted to know if he could cover for him. He had been out of the office all day at a comic book convention that was held in town. He had told his boss he was consulting with him about a project their two companies were working on together and wanted to be sure they had the details straight. With one hour and fifteen minutes to live Winston was using up his last day rather foolishly.

As he evaluated his workload, he decided that it was time to get in gear and accomplish something before this day was over. In the next forty minutes, he finished three projects, forwarded or answered seventeen important emails while deleting seventy-five others. One he did not eliminate was from a pajama company. He smiled as he left it on his computer. They might be something to send Donna after their lunch today. He would also send one to his wife. He would charge them both on his one truly personal credit card. He kept it for occasions like this. He could charge something as a surprise for his wife, and she would never know about it because the bill and confirmation email came to his office account. He could also send Donna flowers, and maybe even that cute sleeper set, and no one would be the wiser. He wanted to keep up the romance in his life. Twenty-five minutes and counting. If he only knew what was about to happen. How much different this day might have been.

He started closing up and planning his dash to the bus and the long, annoying ride home. He would get more done on that ride than the rest of the day. It was his real office. An Emergency alert text message came in telling him his favorite player was injured and his fantasy team would be without him for the rest of the season. He let out a profanity followed by, "Now that has got to be the worst thing that could happen to me today. I thought it was going to be a good day, but nooooo… he has to go and ride a motorcycle into the side of a tree and mess up my whole fantasy season." He only thought that was the worst thing that could happen to him. Winston was on a collision course with death and meeting his Maker. He headed toward the door as the other employees in the office hustled out too. They smiled, nodded and all walked toward the door. Five minutes and thirty-four seconds can be a lifetime if it is all you have left to live.

AN APPOINTMENT TO KEEP

It is appointed for men to die once and after this comes judgment. Hebrews 9.27

Death is neither a friend nor an enemy. Death is always coming until it gets here. It seems to always come too soon or at an extremely inconvenient time and it interrupts plans people have made believing they have plenty of life left. Death for some is a door, and for others, it is the end because they think there is nothing on the other side. Yet, the truth for everyone, death is an appointment we are destined to keep, some sooner than others. We may choose to make it come sooner through ignorance and bad decisions or then again through caution and care, a person may delay it for some undetermined period of time, but death is always coming. It sometimes comes so suddenly as to jolt the human soul and make all who see it pull back in fear. Winston James Cummings is about to have one of those moments that people will talk about for the rest of their lives. He has two minutes to live as he descends the stairs of his building. The time will fly by, but it will be all the life that is left for him. Winston steps out of the building and moves quickly toward the bus stop forty feet from the door.

If time could be frozen, you would see the events, and everyone involved in what is about to happen. Stopping time would put it into its proper perspective. People and events that occur over and over and on that one day, the timing is a little different and what would have been an ordinary day becomes the most memorable day in a person's life.

There is the homeless drug addict who wants to get into the doorstep right after the last person leaves the building. He knows, like so many other homeless, that this door leaks warm air that helps keep whoever can get there first warm through the night. There is the plump 27-year-old office worker, Bridget, who has such an aversion to street people she can become physically ill if one bumps into her. She is afraid she will catch some disease and suffer a slow horrible death. She gets a fresh cup of coffee from the office machine before she leaves work to drink on the ride home. It saves her several dollars a day, and she still gets her caffeine fix. There is the bus driver who has driven this route for three years. She does not speed, but she also does not stop or slow down any sooner than she has to. The routine of city traffic does not leave any room for kindness. People cut her off on an hourly basis. She has the stopping of the bus down to a fraction of a second. A fully loaded city bus weighs around 44,000 lbs. Even at 20 mph has a stopping distance of almost 30 feet but that is only if the driver has a perfect reaction time. Then there is Winston who played football from the time he could and was a star running back in high school and played the first two years of college till he tweaked his knee and buckled down and got a degree. He still has fast reflexes and responds without thinking when something happens near him. The running back in him does not want to get tackled or hit. He does not think about it when his reflexes kick in, and he jumps out of the way. Today that response will be the worst thing he could do, but that is out of his control. He now has less than sixty seconds till he will discover if death is a door or the end of it all.

Slow motion is not how life happens but to see everything clearly we will reduce his last sixty seconds into small pictures. Winston steps out of the doorway and starts toward the bus stop as he has done day after day for the ten years he has worked in this building. He dodges people and maneuvers' through the crowded sidewalk and unto the bus like a linebacker dodging and weaving, headed toward the goal line. At the same time, Bridget comes up the walk carrying her cup of coffee. She is watching the sidewalk in front of her, not wanting to step into any puddles with her new boots. She has saved for six months to be able to afford them. Right now, she is following a man in a long raincoat with a wide brim hat.

The homeless drug addict is pushing his way through the crowded street as the next bus approaches. His goal to be on the step the moment the door is locked so he can stay warm throughout the night. He is not the only one who uses this, and it is first come, first serve. He pushes through the crowd right into the path of Bridget who sees his unshaven face, tattered army jacket and at the same moment smells his perfuse body odor. He is inches from her when she sees him come between her and the man she has been following. Quickly she jumps back and as she screams her fear causes her to toss the cup of coffee to her side. Winston has just entered the area and out of the corner of his eye sees a large cup of coffee headed his way and his reflexes kick in. There were no thoughts about what to do next. He has a lifetime of avoiding being tackled that causes him to jump back and to his left, across the curb and right into the path of the bus. The driver is at that moment was looking at her side mirror to check the traffic beside her. She only took her eyes off the road for a second or two. Winston has leaped into the street and is inches from the front of the bus suspended in the air. At that moment the driver looked up, and instead of slamming on the brakes of the bus she merely breathes out three words, "Oh, God NO!" and then finally moves to slam on the brakes, but before she can get them pressed the 44,000 lbs. of the bus and passengers plow into Winston.

The human body is extremely flexible and resilient but was never designed to be hit by anything that big or going that fast. Winston's body is instantly compressed as it flattens against the grill of the bus and then thrown forward. The damage is extreme as his crumpled and flailing body shoots forward, but the accident is not over, and the damage to his body is not yet complete. As he flies forward, he is launched into the back of a large pickup truck with a topper on the back. He bounces off it, and the broken body falls like a discarded rag doll between the bus and the truck as the bus covers him and rams into the back of the truck. The sound of bones breaking, tires squealing, glass breaking, and gasps followed by Bridget's blood-curdling scream and then for 10 seconds absolute silence as everyone stares. The city around this scene moves on, but everyone here is frozen, everyone except the homeless man who has seized the opportunity to grab his spot on the doorstep where he plans to spend the night. He is unaware of all that has happened, but for tonight he has a warm place and does not care about anything else.

Everyone who has seen the accident or who sees

the results will never forget the sight, the sounds, and even the smell of the bus tires and brakes. Inside the bus, passengers are thrown forward. Several have bumps and bruises while others are shouting profanities at the driver. The driver has broken into tears burying her head in her arms on the steering wheel. The people on the sidewalk are turning away as a pool of blood forms around Winston's crumpled body as it lays under the front of the bus. Bridget composed herself and hurried away unaware that it was her cup of coffee that cost a man his life. All she wanted to do is get away from the homeless man who, for a brief moment, had been inside of her safety zone. She is hurrying home to take a bath as she turns the corner to catch the bus on her alternate route one block away. It will take her fifteen minutes longer on this route, but the bus in front of her office was not going to be moving for some time.

The 911 switchboard lit up suddenly as everyone grabbed their phones to either call or video what had happened. The calls were urgent and convoluted as people regained their senses and began to realize what had really happened.

The squealing tires and the piercing scream had caught the attention of the fire unit at the red light. They were across the street. They turned on their lights and brought the firetruck across the street blocking all four lanes. They were on their way back from another call to deal with a homeless man passed out in a local park used by drug addicts. Two police officers on bikes saw the fire truck light up and blow its horn to clear the way and responded from the other direction less than two blocks away. In a few moments, it had gone from an ordinary day to a street filled with police, paramedics, and people either pushing forward to see what was going on or shoving their way around the scene as they worked to get home. Traffic backed up throughout the city as the accident caused a ripple effect that would take five hours to clear. They all worked in rapid and well-rehearsed fashion to get to Winston's body. Not knowing the extent of the internal injuries, they got his body out and began emergency resuscitation. Winston had no pulse, was not breathing and his eyes were fixed and fully dilated. The crowd watched as they worked to restore life to the broken body. The computer hook-up to the hospital was down, and they continued to apply CPR and other measures to try and restore life. Winston was dead, but they had other plans and were not giving up on life-saving measures.

CROSSING OVER

*Do not boast about tomorrow,
for you do not know what
a day may bring forth.* ^{Proverbs 27.1}

It happened so fast that Winston was one moment walking, the next avoiding a flying cup of coffee. Then for a brief moment, he was looking directly at a bus driver with her wide open and horrified eyes. He heard his body hit the bus and the sound of the tires. He felt the motion as he flew forward into the truck, yet there was no pain. It all happened so fast the number of pain receptors that sent messages to his brain caused an instant overload, so the brain stopped receiving or accepting any new pain impulses. It was as close to an out of body experience as you can get and still be alive, but then again, he was no longer alive.

Winston opened his eyes and looked around. It was dark, and as he tried to focus, he saw a faint light in the distance. It was almost like the very first rays of the sun coming up except there was no horizon, just light in the distance. He was trying to get his bearings. Everything felt different, almost surreal. His mind was in a grey fog. He shook his head a little and rubbed his eyes to get them to clear up. He felt no pain and was completely confused. He knew he had been hit by a bus. The last thing he clearly remembered was the eyes of the bus driver and reading her lips saying 'God…NO!'

The fog began to clear, and he looked around. In one direction it was complete darkness. In the other direction, he saw some light in the distance and began to be aware he was not alone. He could not see anyone in particular, but he sensed there were others. They were moving toward the light and away from the darkness. He held out his arm and slowly turned around feeling his way in the dark. The side toward the light was crisp and cool. It felt good and refreshing. As he turned, his arm came into the darkness and felt it hanging there like a shroud or curtain right behind him. He pushed his hand against it and found it was solid after a few inches. This seemed strange because as he did this, he saw a woman walking toward him. He could see her as a grey ghost deep in the darkness headed in his direction. He expected her to walk into the wall he could feel, but she walked right past him. She did not speak or act like she even saw Winston. He took a few steps forward and stopped again. He had the strangest feeling he was being followed. Nothing was there. He stepped back toward the darkness and ran smack into the wall of darkness. Only it had moved. It was as if it was following him. He turned and walked forward twenty or thirty feet, and when he turned back, the wall was right behind him. Another person appeared, a small girl wearing jeans and a red striped t-shirt. She looked to be about eight years old.

As she passed by, she smiled and then asked Winston if this was the right way to go. He nodded, and she moved on away from him and toward the light. He watched for several minutes as she walked away and grew smaller and smaller. Then he began to walk slowly forward into a gray light that glowed through the dense fog it became lighter, he could see people walking in the same general direction he was. They all seemed to, be headed toward the same place and as they moved forward, they were also getting closer together, even though the distance between them was immense. He looked back, and people were coming out of the darkness all over the place. One man in shorts and a tank top was running forward and flew past him. A lady had stopped and was standing still. As he approached, she spoke to him.

"Do you know where we are? I don't know how I got here."

Winston stopped and stared at her. He did not know where this was either. "Sorry, I'm not sure. What is the last thing you remember before being here?"

She looked down and then back up. I was teaching in my high school class when…" She grew quiet before continuing. "Mark Cobb came into the room and was screaming at me that he had lost his scholarship because of me. I had flunked him. He only came to my English class twice all year and wanted me to pass him because he was a star forward on the basketball team. We have metal detectors at our school to stop guns from getting in. The teachers had asked to be allowed to have guns, but some state senator had pushed through a bill that made a teacher with a firearm in school a felony. That same senator has an armed bodyguard. Mark pulled a knife. It was not medal, but a composite I would guess. He came at me and.. and… He was stabbing me over and over. I was screaming for help. The students were all running out of the classroom. I fell to the floor, and he got on top and kept stabbing me, over and over… and… here I am."

She looked down at herself expecting to see blood and wounds. "I don't understand." She repeated it and started walking toward the light. She stopped, turned back holding out her hands with the palms up and slowly rotating them. She kept looking at her hands and her stomach. "This is so surreal, completely unbelievably, where is the blood?" Then she turned and walked toward the light again.

Winston felt someone take his hand. He did not pull away; he turned and looked down. It was a boy about 4 or 5 years old. He did not speak and started walking holding tight to his hand. So, Winston walked along for a few minutes. Then the boy let go and walked away toward the light. Winston stood there with people passing by.

It was slowly getting a little lighter as they walked on. A man had stopped a few feet away and was facing toward those walking out of the darkness. He had his hand out and just kept saying over and over. "NO…NO…NO…" He seemed to be pushing against something, but Winston saw nothing. "I don't want to be here, and I can't go back." He spoke to Winston. "There is a wall that is following me, and it will not let me go back.

Winston stretched out his arm toward where the man was pushing and felt nothing. Then he turned and stretched out his arm toward the darkness. The wall was there for him too. He had his own wall following him. "We don't seem to have any choice in the matter. We have to go forward, and we don't seem to be able to go back."

The man looked at Winston and then sat down. "I am not going any further. I don't want to be here. I have my whole life in front of me, and this is not how I planned for things to go. Besides, this cannot be real. There is no scientific proof there is life after death. I have studied it, and there is no such thing as God. No sir, I am going to wait here till I wake up from this terrible experience and whatever I did to cause this to happen, I promise I will never do it or eat it again."

Winston turned and started walking with the ever-growing number of people. The open path began to change, and people started to walk in lines. It was not as if they were following each other, but somehow, they were being confined or funneled to these lines. In a short time, he realized he was on a walkway that resembled a clear marble surface but was almost translucent. Others were walking with him. He could hear people talking, others crying and even a few were cursing. He felt so very much different than he had ever felt before. As he continued, he saw there was a line of people a short distance on the same walkway in front of him. There was a gap between him and them. They were all walking in the same direction he was. He called to them, but they did not turn around and continued to walk on at a steady pace. He started to walk a little faster to catch up and find out where he was when he heard someone speak from behind him.

He turned around and saw a young girl coming toward him. She was in a wheelchair. She was smiling as she drew closer to him. Her legs were visible, or what legs she had. They were very thin and shriveled, and her two feet were both resting on one-foot pad together because they were so small and useless. She pumped the wheels as she approached like she was well experienced in using the wheelchair. She came straight at him at breakneck speed and then swerved at the last second, spinning around him and coming to a sudden stop in front of Winston.

Nancy Parker Criss had been born with a series of congenital disabilities and was not expected to live the first week. Then it was the first month, year, and finally, the doctors quit guessing and worked to help her live a better life. She was confined to a wheelchair, had to have oxygen 24/7 and had spent more of her life in the hospital than anywhere else. School for her was only a way to socialize as she missed too much of her classes ever really to get a grade. She was brilliant and loved to read. She devoured books from the school library and on her unlimited electronic subscription. It allowed her to escape when she could not be in class with the other kids. She was a member of the local Independent Christian Fellowship church. When she was not able to attend, she would watch the service online with the live feed. The church was small, about 50 people on an average Sunday, and she was one of only three young people, but she loved it.

Early this morning she started having trouble breathing, and her parents had rushed her to the hospital. Her mom, Karman, was a member of the church, a committed believer having made a personal commitment at a youth camp as a teenager. She was as active as possible with all the responsibility of caring for Nancy. Her father, Martin, was a welder who worked at the local shipyard and attended church on Christmas Sunday each year. He had grown up in a home without any religion at all and found it hard to understand all the fuss about attending church. Part of the problem may have also been the only Sunday he participated in each year was a children's program retelling the story of the birth of the baby Jesus and did not ever get to the reason for the birth or what it meant for him. He could not understand a God who would allow something like what Nancy was going through to happen. If God was so great and powerful where was

He when his daughter was born.

As the day wore on Pastor Jim was called, and the prayer chain was notified to pray for Nancy. The prayer chain was headed up by Sister Stella. She was in her late 80's and had been part of the church since it was founded thirty-five years ago. She was as spry as they come and would alert the church prayer chain as soon as she got the notice.

The doctors worked feverishly to stabilize Nancy, but her condition deteriorated throughout the day. Late in the day, the doctors told the family there was nothing else they could do, and it looked like she would not make it through the night. They had recommended some drugs in case she was in pain, but Karmen would not have it. She wanted to be able to communicate with her daughter. Karmen, Martin, Pastor Jim, along with Nancy's grandparents on her mom's side, had come into the room as the doctors pulled back allowing them to spend time with Nancy. Her breathing was labored, and her frail body quivered every few minutes.

Pastor Jim gathered the family around the bed and prayed for Nancy and the family. As he did Nancy opened her eyes and smiled weakly.

"Thanks, pastor." Her raspy voice brought tears to everyone's eyes.

"Pastor, do you see them?"

"See what, Nancy? What are we looking at?

"Pastor, there are angels in the room. They are all around you guys."

Pastor Jim looked around, then back at Nancy. "Sorry, I don't, but I bet they aren't here for me to see."

Nancy's mom stepped closer, and the pastor moved back out of the way.

"Mom, they are beautiful. I wish you could see

them." Her eyes were sparkling as she talked about them.

"Pastor is right; they are here for you."

Her father stepped back and turned away. He was struggling with the whole thing. He loved his daughter and was not handling this well. He wanted to cry and at the same time did not want to give in to his emotions. He stepped toward the door past Karmen's parents. They were both believers and attended the church with Karmen and Nancy. The room lights were dimmed except for the one right over Nancy's bed. Martin was in a darkened corner of the room under the TV which had never been turned on. Then he did something he had never done before. He started to pray. It was not audible, it was deep inside, as the tears rolled down his face and his nose began to run. He sniffed deeply and continued to pray. "Please God, I know I have not ever talked to you before, but tonight I need to know you are real and that you can hear me." He stopped praying for a moment as he worked to control his emotions. It did not work; the tears would not stop coming.

Nancy had been right. The room filled with angels. Most people never see them, but they are everywhere. People often see the physical world as the real world, but it is the other way around. The physical world is the shadow of the spiritual world. The physical world is temporary and will pass away. Most people have one guardian angel assigned to them, but they are not allowed to interfere except in rare cases. God's rule of free will and self-determination limits what they are allowed to do.

Nancy's angel had been busy since before Nancy was born and tonight, he was joined by a host of angels, many of which had helped Nancy at various times in her life. There were so many that if those in the room could have seen they would have viewed a room filled with angels that overflowed into the hospital hallway.

As Martin prayed, two angels stood with him. They had their hands on his shoulders, and each of them was also crying as they heard his first prayer ever.

"God, please take me instead. Heal Nancy, Please…" He began to sob as he begged God to hear his first prayer. He could not hold it in any longer. Carl, Nancy's grandfather, stepped forward and gathered his son-in-law in his arms and held him tight as he began to pray out loud.

"God, please heal Nancy. You choose how, but please be here with us tonight." The angles were all smiling as they understood this prayer of faith which transcended time and space. This was not a selfish prayer for the people in the room but a prayer for Nancy. The little girl had struggled and suffered her whole life, but she had never complained or blamed anyone. Healing, final real healing, was not physical and temporary but spiritual and would not happen in this world. Real healing was the resurrection into eternal life and the receiving of a new body.

Martin wrapped his arms around his father-in-law. They had never been close but tonight barriers were all gone. Here was the father he needed to hold him close and he sobbed into his shoulder as the angels reached out to touch him and lift their voices in unison agreeing with Carl's prayer. Their prayer of "Yes Lord," reverberated throughout the heavens to the throne of God.

"Dad." It was Nancy calling her father. "Dad." Her voice was clear and robust.

Everyone looked toward Martin as he turned and moved toward the other side of the bed. He took her hand and tried to wipe the tears from his eyes.

"Dad, he heard. He is going to heal me. This is the greatest day of my life. I love you, dad." She breathed deeply, then continued. "Thanks for praying for me, Dad. I have been praying for you for years."

Martin looked at his daughter. She was smiling at him and looked so peaceful. He felt a peace inside he had never experienced before.

"Mom, I love you."

Karmen mouthed the words, "I Love You." Tears were running down her cheeks. She stood on the other side of the bed from Martin holding Nancy's other hand.

The machine beside the bed began to beep. The nurse moved and turned it off.

Nancy looked down toward the end of the bed where her grandparents stood. Both with tears in their eyes. She smiled at them and then closed her eyes. She was gone.

Martin looked toward Pastor Jim. "Would you pray for us please." Not words he would typically have spoken but his life had changed. He wanted to answer his daughter's prayers. The angels in the room began to applaud and rejoice. It was a room full of miracles. The body of Nancy lay motionless; she was gone.

Nancy spun the wheelchair around in front of Winston. "Wow isn't this great?" she asked with an excited and happy voice. She smiled and then continued. "I have looked forward to this my whole life. I mean this is everything I was hoping and more."

Winston stared at her for a moment, not saying

anything as he thought of how ironic it was that someone in a wheelchair was excited to be here. Wherever here was.

"Don't you agree?" she said with the smile that never seemed to fade. Her eyes sparkled, and she was bubbling over with happiness.

Winston had been caught off guard at first. He was still trying to adjust to all that was happening but now kneeled in front of her. "Tell me, how did you get here?"

"Oh, I have always been sick. I was born early. My mom was the best. She always took the best care of me. I started having trouble breathing and had to go to the hospital. It was a long day, but here I am. This is absolutely the best I have ever felt in the whole fourteen years of my life. I can breathe clearly, and my energy has never been this high. I mean, this is absolutely the best day of my life. I don't need an oxygen tube for the first time in.. well, forever!" She stopped, spun her wheelchair around and pulled it right up to Winston.

Now he was smiling. Her smile was contagious, and he had caught it.

Then she continued. "I have been looking forward to this since I was ten and went to the summer camp sponsored by our church. My mom was worried and did not want me to go, but I got her to give in. Well kinda give in. She went along. That was the best summer of my life. I remember that was when I surrendered my life to the Master. It took ten guys carrying me and the wheelchair into the lake so that I could get baptized. I did get sick, and it took two months to get better, but it was worth it."

She rolled back away from him. "Nice talking hope

to see you later. I want to see where we are going. Can't go back, the wall and all, you know. Bye." And she spun around a couple of times, smiling all the while and took off in a sideward direction toward some others in the distance. She flew off the ramp and kept right on going. She was flying or gliding. She moved like she was on a solid surface, but there was nothing under her.

He was not sure how long he had been standing there before he brought his thoughts back into focus and looked around. People were coming and going. Coming out of the darkness and walking toward the light. As he walked, he saw an older black woman who was standing still, looking back toward the darkness with a worried look on her face. As he approached, she reached out to stop him.

"Have you seen Charles?" She asked with a kind and worried voice.

"Who? I mean I don't think I know who Charles is." He started to walk on, but she grabbed on to his arm.

She spoke with a raspy voice. "You would know him if you saw him. He is well, first he is black, but his hair is white. He is old like me. We have been together for 83 years now. We dated in high school and got married the summer after he graduated. I was a year behind him and had to wait until I turned eighteen. We have been married to each other for 79 years. Got married in the church and attended every Sunday since then. Charles and I are best friends. He is a deacon in the church and teaches a Sunday School class for the younger folks. You know those people in their 50's and 60's. Where is he? I have never slept a night away from him in all those years. In fact, I was having trouble sleeping so I went out on the porch to get some fresh air. I sat down in the rocker and fell asleep. Then I woke up here. I have been walking slow. I know when he finds I am gone he will catch up." She stopped talking and looked back toward the darkness. "I would go find him but there is this wall following me, and I can't go back. Could you go back and check and see where he is? I will wait right here for you and him." Her eyes showed the concern and lostness of being anywhere without her husband and best friend.

"I would, but I can't," Winston said with a gesture toward the darkness stretching out his arm and pushing against the invisible wall. "I have one of those walls too. It lets me go forward but not backward. This is a big place. It might be best if you went on and let him catch up. It seems we are all headed in the same direction." He was now holding her hands in his and looking down into her eyes.

"No, I better wait. You go on. Thanks for listening. I know he will be along shortly." She patted his hand and shuffled to one side. She was smiling at Winston, but tears were welling up in her eyes. "Now go on young man, don't let me stop you. I will wait here for Charles." She smiled and waved weakly at him.

"What is your name if I see him so I can tell him where you are?

"I'm Rina Mae, and I will wait here because I know he would not go on without me." She folded her arms across her chest and strained to look into the darkness hoping to see Charles.

He wanted to get her to go on, but he somehow knew it was not going to happen. He walked away, and she stayed there watching him. There was no distance or perception of space. The only thing he could see were the people as they came and went. Even those who walked away from him seemed to disappear rather quickly. They seemed to fade out when they got a distance from him. If he walked faster, they reappeared. It was getting lighter, and when he looked back, the darkness was fading. It was pleasant walking, and he was not getting tired and was not hungry or thirsty.

Two men approached from different paths. The one was short, plump and balding. He wore a suit and tie and had an air about him. The other one was a short man of Chinese descent. He was wearing village clothes and was walking with a limp. They both came to a stop right in front of Winston. The small Chinese man smiled and bowed, then rose and offered his hand to Winston. "I am pastor Xi of the New Hope Saviors Church."

The other man smiled and introduced himself. "I am the Dr. Reverend Roger Capps Jr. I am a member of the Mason County General Assembly King James Baptist Church. I am delighted to meet you."

Winston looked at the two men and decided he might as well introduce himself too. "I am Winston, and I am not a pastor. This is the first time I have ever been in the presence of two pastors at the same time. I must be in double trouble." He smiled at his little joke. The Chinese pastor smiled, and the American pastor wrinkled his brow and stared at him.

Winston broke the silence. "Well, how did you get here?

Reverend Capps spoke first. I was at a church dinner eating fried chicken when I began to choke. I am an evangelist I had finished a revival service where I, personally, lead fifteen people to join the local church over the weekend. I was planning on taking a vacation down on the gulf with my wife tomorrow to celebrate. I have been pastoring for thirty-five years and have three degrees. I have led hundreds to join the local church. I can hardly wait to see how that puts jewels in my crown."

Winston and Pastor Xi stood there as Reverend Capps rambled on about himself and all his personal accomplishments. Reverend Capps finally stopped, and Winston turned toward Pastor Xi.

He had never stopped smiling and occasionally bowing. Now he looked up at Winston and spoke. "I was locked up five years ago for running an illegal underground church. It was the third time this has happened. Once I was held under house arrest for a whole year. They took all our Bibles, and our children were taken to a mind modification project where they were taught the benefits of communism and its answers to the world's problems. While in prison I was responsible for moving rocks from one stack to another all day, every day. Summer or winter it did not matter. All I had was the clothes I was issued on the first day. I was so glad I had memorized scripture. I was able to recite it over and over as I moved those rocks. I wanted to talk to the guards, but I never had the same guards two days in a row. I had been sharing with them about my faith, and several of them got saved, so they were not allowed to talk to me and were changed every day. They wanted me to renounce my faith and promised my children would be brought back if I did. I refused, and the guard started beating me. I don't remember much after that except waking up here, walking in the darkness.

Winston could not help but take in the difference between these two men. Both were ministers, but that is where it all ended. The one was focused on his accomplishments while the other one focused on his ministry for the Lord.

The two men both started on again. Reverend Capps was talking about his accomplishments as they went and the Chinese pastor nodding his head in agreement and smiling. It was not like he was listening. He seemed to be taking in where he was and how much better it was here than where he had spent most of the last thirty years.

First Contact

***But the angel of the LORD called to him
from heaven and said, "Abraham, Abraham!"
And he said, "Here I am." Genesis 22.11***

"Winston wait, I need to talk to you." a clear and very masculine voice was speaking to him. Winston looked around, and there was a very tall being. He would have called him a man, but something was wrong. The guy was tall. At least 7 foot or even taller and he had huge wings tucked tight against his back. They extended above his head and almost to the floor, on any other day that might have seemed strange but somehow today that was exactly what he was expecting. Winston stopped and stared at the being. Maybe what he needed to do is take the guy's advice and sit down and wait until he woke up. This was the weirdest, most real dream he had ever had.

"You have caused quite a stir here today." He spoke to Winston again.

Winston was somehow aware this was not a dream but some new reality he had entered. The being before him did not frighten him, but at the same time, he was aware of the power and majesty of the being or person or thing who was speaking to him.

"Where am I, who are you? What happened? How did I get here?" Winston rattled of the string of questions so fast he even surprised himself. "Who are you, no, what are you..?" He started to speak again but the being held up his hand in a motion to stop asking questions, narrowed his eyes and spoke again.

"First you are at the eternal separation and

45

departure sanctuary. I know you don't know what that means, but it will be explained to you shortly. I need you to follow directions and come with me. We have some things to sort out. Either you are not supposed to be here yet, or you got here a little too soon. By the way, I am Marcos, and I have been assigned to get you through this situation." The being turned and started walking and as he did, he began to disappear into the grey mist along a new walkway that had appeared.

Winston stood there stunned. His mind was spinning and having trouble focusing. He was where? Did he say his name was Marcos? Did that guy really have wings? What the h…

"Winston, you need to keep up," came the call from the mist in front of him.

He started walking quickly and suddenly realized how clearly all his senses were working. He never in all his life had felt so much transparency within his being. He looked at his hands as he walked and was amazed at how good he felt. He was moving his fingers around when wham he walked right into the wings of Marcos who glanced back with a look that showed he did not appreciate Winston running into him.

He stepped back and looked around. The mist was gone. There was now no up or down. Things were happening on levels all around him in every conceivable and non-conceivable direction. As he looked toward the horizon, there were lines of people that seemed to stretch forever. There were lines of people above him that appeared to be upside down. All these lines headed in the same basic direction. Some were straight, some curved like ribbons and on each of them were people walking. Some lines were full, and others only had a few in them, but they all were lines of people. Marcos stopped and smiled before he spoke as Winston looked at the lines.

"With almost 8 billion people in the world, about 55 million people die each year from an unlimited and varied set of causes. That averages out to about 154 thousand people a day who die around the world and end up here. That does not include when a war breaks out, or a plague or national disaster kills a group suddenly. Then the lines are longer. Every one of them has to be processed and delivered to their proper and personally preselected locations. Those lines are a non-stop process that will not come to an end until the end of time. When that day comes about half of the total population that has ever lived will be judged, and then this place will shut down and disappear."

Winston was stunned, and then it hit him. He slowly turned around and looked in every direction. "Those people are dead…?" It was a question, statement, and realization all at once. As he looked around the lines, they all came in from one side toward the other of the vast expanse. They came from up high and down low and seemed to merge into each other as they moved across the one vast area. One side of the expanse was grey and foggy and had no clear definition. It was here the lines started. People would appear as small spots out of the mist or fog walking on one of the paths or bridges while the other side of the expanse was bright white and smooth. He repeated his comment or question in a much softer voice and directed it to Marcos. "Are those people dead?"

"Yes, and yes, since you now realize or should have realized it, you are dead too." He stopped speaking and waited for it to soak in.

"The bus did hit me then?"

"Yes, made a real mess of you, and made a real mess here too." Marcos held up a small clear screen and looked at it for details. "You died and were worked on by a group of fire-fighters and police officers before being transported to the local trauma hospital. You have been dead and resuscitated several times. They are trying to resuscitate you right now. Right now, you are flat lined. Somehow you are here, and it may not be your time. The mind and spirit are not to come here before you are finally dead and ready to appear here. Then you are to get the new body you have now and be processed right through to your personally preselected eternal location. You should be glad we caught this now. You were not at the point of no return." Marcos smiled for the first time. "This could be your lucky day."

"My lucky day? What do you mean my lucky day? You just told me I was hit by a bus and I'm dead, and you are telling me this might be my lucky day? I would hate to see what you called a bad day." Winston was animated, moving his hands and arms. He was scared and confused. He had never thought of what it might be like to be dead. Even at funerals he usually spends time looking at his watch and thinking about his fantasy football team. The only time he had even contemplated his own life was at his father's funeral. Death was what happened to old people, and Winston was not old, but he realized he was dead. Now, and for the first time, he was afraid, confused and wished he had sat down with the other guy in the mist and waited.

"Look around you. This place is full of people, and the majority are about to have the worst day of their lives. Now, here is what you need to know." Marcos spoke calmly and in a quiet voice to Winston. Winston suddenly realized there were all sorts of people and beings around him in all directions, yet, it was hushed and peaceful. "It happens about once every thousand years, or so someone gets here early. Now everyone ends up coming through this place, but very few get here early. If this were your time for sure, you would be in one of those lines headed toward the Crown Court where you would learn where you are going to spend eternity."

Winston interrupted speaking rapidly, "Crown Court? Forever? NO, NO, NO... I, I, I..." he was stammering, and his mind was spinning. He thought everyone went to heaven when they died, or if Marsha, one of his secretaries in his office, who had studied Hinduism was right, you were translated into a new body working your way up toward the mind of God and perfection. This is not what he expected. He had listened to a preacher on television recently talking about our eternal home. He had preached about happiness and personal wealth. This preacher had a personal jet and a large house. He told the audience that God's plan was all about riches. There was no need to get down on your knees to pray, that was a position the devil loved so he could kick your butt. It was the first preacher Winston had liked and laughed as he made fun of what were called 'panty-wasted believers.' He liked the preacher right up until he started that "send in your gift" stuff. He had made it sound like everyone went to heaven. What about those books written by people who go to heaven and come back? How could that be true if this place existed?

"So, what happens now? Will I go back and get my body back or will I get a new one like the guys in the movies do when a mistake is made. Will I be able to play the saxophone?" Winston rambled off a string of questions for Marcos. "Will the people back there know me when I get there? How long will it take? Can I pick my body or will…"

"Winston" Marcos interrupted him. "This is not a movie. Forget all that stuff made up by a bunch of people who don't even believe in God. You are my responsibility until it is all sorted out. As far as those movies go, they have nothing to do with reality. Why would you think some guy who never goes to church and wants to entertain people knows anything about what happens after you die? I have some things to take care of, but I will try and answer any questions you may have." Marcos started to move away. He went to the right and upward as he departed. Winston was not sure what to do. That was not a direction he had ever gone before. He stepped out and found that there was a path to follow right behind Marcos. As he followed, he looked around. This place did not go on forever, but the edges were not clearly defined. All the lines came in from the gray mist. The lines all seemed to head in the same direction toward a large wall. He could not see where they ended from where he was standing. He stopped and looked around in disbelief at what he was seeing.

He hurried to catch up. "What happens here exactly?"

"Just keep up, and you will see." Marcos turned and started off again.

Winston followed for what was an excessively long time — passing the lines of people. They were all colors, races, and ages. These people had all died today, and this scene would be repeated every day. He had never thought of the process of dealing with all the souls as they passed from life to death. "Marcos, this body looks like mine, but it feels different," Winston spoke hoping for some more information.

"Everyone gets a new body when they die. These bodies are different. This is your resurrection from the dead. The body that is sown is perishable, it is raised imperishable; it is sown in dishonor, it is raised in glory; it is sown in weakness, it is raised in power; it is sown a natural body, it is raised a spiritual body. If there is a natural body, there is also a spiritual body.[3] Today is your resurrection from the dead, and you have your new spiritual body. It will continue to change as you go through this process until you get to the Crown Court, by then the transformation will be complete. The key is, it is an eternal body. It will not decay or ever wear out. It does not get sick, and you will never die. You have all of your senses, and they work better than they ever did in your physical earthly body. All the people you saw have their new eternal spiritual bodies and, like you, are adjusting to them. Part of the process is looking the same when you first get here so you can understand what is happening and be a little more comfortable. You will continue to change as you go through the process right up to the final moments here."

"How long does that take?" he said hurrying to get closer to Marcos as they moved, walked, floated or whatever it was they were doing.

Marcos stopped and turned back toward Winston. "You have it all wrong. You asked, 'How long?' There is no time here. There can be no time here. This is forever. Clocks don't exist. Time is how you measure something that can be measured. Time is how you measure your life. You measure it from when you were born. You measure time to try and understand life and give it meaning. There is nothing here to measure. Forever is forever and ever and that is longer than time will ever be." He drew closer and put his hand on Winston's shoulder. "You have not been to the judgment yet, but for your sake, I pray you are ready. If not, forever will be the worst experience that will go on and on. There are only two ways this goes. There is eternal life, and there is eternal punishment.[4] That message is so important that when the Master was on earth in his human body, he made sure to warn everyone. He made sure it was written in the book you call the New Testament. Now, beyond that, there are rewards in eternal life, and it may be hard to believe but Dante was right about levels or as he called them circles of hell or eternal punishment, but he was far too kind to those who do not make it to eternal life. The truth is when you think it can't get any worse it can and for many, it will, forever. Got it? Good."

Winston stood looking at Marcos with a confused and blank look. Forever somehow sounded different than it had ever before. It was in many ways too much to take in. Then he looked around. Far below were the lines. He could see them moving but was not sure where they were coming from or where they were going. "So, if, say, well…" Winston was afraid to ask the question, but he wanted the answer. "How long do you stay in hell if you get sent there?"

"Remember I told you there is no time here?"

Winston nodded his head.

"It is called eternal punishment and eternal life for a reason. The only way to get eternal life is to accept the sacrifice made by the Master himself. Death is a barrier or finish line that, when crossed, everything is completed and permanent. One life and one lifetime to make the choices where you want to spend eternity. Eternal means just that and nothing less."

Marcos turned and started once again. This time he was headed down, or whatever direction that was, toward the long lines below. Winston was standing there stunned when he heard a stern call from the winged messenger who was not waiting on him. "WINSTON! Keep up. I have responsibilities to take care of." Breaking into a jog, he found himself right beside this being and trying to understand all he had seen and heard so far.

"Wait." Winston stopped and continued. "Are you an angel?"

"Have you noticed the wings?" Marcos smiled and for the first time stretched them out. They were huge, like bird's wings, only different. They were translucent and almost luminous. There were no distinct feathers but ripples that showed variances of colors. The ends were darker like highlights in someone's hair. Then as quickly as he opened them, they were folded. "I don't need them much here, but when I am in the kingdom proper, they are wonderful to use. I don't mind answering your questions, but you have to keep up." Then off he went again.

"How do you become an angel, anyway? Is it a promotion people get when they have been here awhile?" Somehow Winston had moved on from the reason all these people were here and the eternal life and punishment to a curiosity of what was happening around him.

"No, it is not a promotion. It is how I was created. I have always been an angel, and I will always be one. I serve the one true living God. Unlike you, I have no eternal soul given me by God. He breathed life into Adam that was the essence of His being. When it says that man was created in the image of God, it is not just how he looks. Man, like God, has three parts. One part is perishable and left behind when you die. That is your body. So, you get a new eternal one."

As they continued to move forward, Marcos slowed and turned to Winston giving him new directions. "Stay close to me and keep your voice down. I have to take care of a situation that has developed. This happens several times a day."

The lines were all around them. The people's faces showed every emotion imaginable. Some were crying for joy and others were crying in fear. Some stared straight ahead while others were looking around trying to figure it all out. The lines came up to angels who spoke softly and guided the people into new lines. Most of the lines merged but occasionally someone was sent to a new line or was put in a line by themselves. As they approached a line, a man was standing beside a woman. She was engaged in a rather heated argument with the angel who was pointing to a line while the woman was pointing to another one. The angel never raised his voice, but you could tell from the expression on his face; this was growing old.

Marcos approached the angel as the woman continued to raise her voice and demand to see the person in charge right now.

"She has not stopped once and will not listen to a word I say to her. She keeps screaming; she should not be here and wants to see, 'the woman in charge.' I am quoting her." The angel was shaking his head from side to side as Marcos stepped around patting him on his shoulder and approached the woman.

"I will take care of this, and you get things back on track." Marcos spread out his wings and pushed toward the woman.

"So, you want to see the person in charge?" Marcos asked in a mocking voice. For an angel, he could have some attitude and was one for the quick answer. He towered over her as he folded his wings and continued, "I seriously doubt you want to see who is in charge. You have no idea what is about to happen here. I am not your judge, but from what I can see, the life about to be judged was not happy. You think being loud is akin to being in charge and getting your way. So why don't you tell me exactly what you think is going on here and I will see if I can't get it all straightened out." Everyone in the lines nearby was watching, and the lines in that area were barely moving. It was like a wreck on the freeway at rush hour except here everyone in these lines was dead. Everyone slowed down to see what happened and everything eventually comes to a complete stop, even in the lanes without any problems. It was as if they had forgotten where they were and wanted to see what was going to happen next. Some of them were hoping this tactic would work so they could use it too.

Pointing her index finger at Marcos, she was almost screaming, "I have been in church for most of my life, and I know that Mother Sophia runs this place and I want to see her right now!" She was red in the face and acting like yelling would get her whatever she wanted. Her husband was standing behind her with his head down. He was weeping, and his shoulders were trembling. She looked at him and sharply spoke. "Stop that, you worthless little man."

"What happened?" Marcos spoke to him directly.

He looked up and started to speak, but his wife interrupted. She stepped between Marcos and her husband. "I told you I want to see Mother Sophia. I can feel her energy, and I know she wants me to be with her."

"Please, shut up." The husband spoke as he stepped back around to her side. "Don't you see this is not what you think it is. We are in real trouble here…" He turned to Marcos and started talking. "We were in the car, and I was driving. She was telling me what she wanted me to do when we got home. She always tells me what she wants me to do. I was listening to her and not responding. We have been married for thirty-five years. Today I was absolutely too tired of it all and was not responding. She reached over and grabbed my chin and yanked my face toward her. She wanted me to pay attention when she was talking. When she jerked my face, I must have swerved out of my lane so when I looked up. We were on a collision course with a tanker truck full of fuel. She is screaming that I am such an idiot and then WHAM! Then the next thing we are walking in the darkness and she has not stopped telling me this is all my fault and she is going to deal with me as soon as she can get everything straightened out." His wife had turned toward him and was scowling as he talked to the angel. Her hands were on her hips, and her face was turning red.

She did not let him go on but interrupted. "How dare you speak about me that way?" She snapped at him. "My fault. Screw you. I don't know why I married you." He looked away with tears forming in his eyes. "You are the most pathetic human being and poorest excuse for a husband in the history of mankind." She turned toward Marcos. "I told you I want to see

Mother Sophia right now. When I tell her how I have been treated, you will wish you were never born."

Marcos raised his arm and motioned toward the sky. "Madam, I was not born, and I am eternally grateful for the fact that did not happen if it would make me related to you in any way. Just this short meeting here today is longer than I want to know you or anyone with your attitude." Before she could respond to this outburst from Marcos two red angels came swooping in beside the woman. Marcos bent forward and got right in her face. "Madam, I know that you will be greatly surprised shortly." The angels both had four crimson wings with burnt brown tips. Their clothes and skin were a deep red, and their hair was a burnt auburn color. They were impressive and grabbed the woman by her arms and started lifting her off the ramp. She was facing backward as they started to fly off. "You want to see who is in charge and are in a hurry to start eternity? I have the authority to get you to the beginning of the line." The woman had a shocked look on her face as her legs dangled in the air. "Take her to the front. I will be there shortly to handle this personally. Keep her separate from everyone else. No need to make her comfortable or try and explain anything to her. Just let her vent. She will know soon enough what is going on here and who is really in charge. Yes, rudeness has its rewards. Now get her out of here so we can get things back on track." The angels flew off as the woman kicked her legs and screamed. One shoe fell off as they flew into the distance and it seemed to fade from existence as it fell but never landed.

The woman was not finished yet. She started to kick and scream. "Put me down. I want to see Mother

Sophia right now." In a moment she was far off in the distance, and the area returned to a much calmer atmosphere.

Marcos turned toward the husband who had pulled back away from them when the two red angels showed up. "Do you want to join her? I can make it happen. You can be at the front of the line right beside miss 'I want to see who is in charge.'" Marcos was shaking his head as he spoke imitating the woman.

"No, God no, please no. My only request is never to see that woman again as long as I live, or as long as I am dead or whatever. I don't want to see her ever, forever. If that is possible." He stopped and showed he knew that this was now his life and it was forever. "I have put up with her and her Mother Sophia wisdom belief system forever now."

"Then stay here. The chances of you ever seeing her again are eternally slim, and if it happens, things will be very different. But I hope you have made other arrangements, and then you will be guaranteed never to see her again."

The man looked up at Marcos. "That is the reason I have been crying. I grew up in a preacher's home. My dad preached the whole gospel. I went to Sunday school, summer camps, Vacation Bible School and even went to a Bible college for a semester before transferring to a state college so I could be with her. I know the truth, and I have made no preparations to be here. I let my wife run my life, and I went to that church with her and even practiced that mother earth, humanistic wisdom, gnostic crap, even though I knew it was not true. I know exactly what is coming and I am in no hurry to get to the front of this line." He stepped back into line and lowered his head. "I know better than most here what is coming."

Marcos motion to Winston to wait a moment and then stepped forward and began talking to the two angels that were handling the lines. They were both blue and smaller than Marcos. Marcos seemed to be getting order restored. Winston began to look around and saw the people in the line right beside him. There was a woman who smiled at him.

"Isn't this wonderful?" she spoke with excitement in her voice. "I have been so waiting for this. Wow, praise God! Jesus, Jesus, Jesus!!!" she started shouting and jumping up and down, and her whole body shook as she did.

"Please, will you just shut up." A plump man behind her spoke. "I will gladly go to hell if I don't have to listen to her praising God one more minute."

The man next in line was much older and was shaking his head back and forth. He looked at Winston and started to speak to him.

"I had a wife who believed. She dragged the kids and me to church every Sunday without fail. I have heard some of the finest and worst preachers share the message for the forty-five years we were married. It was a promise I made to her before we got married. I would go to church with her. I never believed any of that stuff. I thought when you die you go to sleep, and it was over. I did not see my being any different than the dog in the yard next door. I did not believe in having a soul, or God, or anything like that. My wife died several years ago, and her funeral was the last time I went to church. My son came to the nursing home and tried to get me to make a confession of faith last week. He knew I was dying. I knew I was dying. He looked me in the face with tears in his eyes and asked me to believe. He said it was not too late. I just said no. I told him the stupid poem that atheist repeat.

'When you die you are just like Rover,
When he died, he died all over.'

I would give anything for five minutes to make it right. I know enough from all that preaching to be sure there are no second opportunities where we are." He stopped talking, and a tear ran down his cheek. After a long pause, he continued. "It is ironic. I will be buried on top of her in our plot, but she went up, and I am going down." He turned and started walking to catch back up to the person in front of him. He glanced back at Winston, and the look in his eyes was sorrow, regret, and fear.

Marcos returned shortly. Winston had heard from several more in the line and was amazed that the majority in this line knew the truth but were not ready. The one exception was the happy lady who was driving the rest of the line crazy.

"They know she is telling the truth and just like in life they don't want to hear it. Even with all the truth of this place staring them in the face they cannot stand to hear the truth because it only reinforces the fact that they are not ready." Marcos finished and touched Winston on the shoulder. "Are you ready to go?"

Winston jumped back a little. "Wait! I thought you said it might not be my time?" He continued to back away from Marcos.

"No, I mean are you ready to go with me? I have some business to take care of. That lady screaming to see who is in charge is waiting on us."

"Oh, well yes, I guess, let's go then." He had been shocked into the reality that this could be his fate and he was sure he did not want this to be his judgment day.

As they started up, there was a commotion that brought everything to a stop. A new path formed and grew. It was different from the rest. No one was on it, but it came from the mist and formed or materialized and stretched across the vast expanse toward the far side where all the lines seemed to merge.

THE TRIUMPHAL ENTRY

"At that time the kingdom of heaven will be like ten virgins who took their lamps and went out to meet the bridegroom. Five of them were foolish and five were wise. Matthew 25.1-2

One man appeared walking gradually forward on the new path. The path he was on was glowing gold and bright. Several angels left their current positions and flew toward him as he walked. Then another man appeared followed by a woman and a child walking from the mist toward the first man. He had stopped and was talking to the angels. It was then Winston looked carefully and saw that he was dark skinned with a middle eastern or Arabic look to his features. In the end, there were five of them standing, talking to the angels. There were three men, a woman and a child about seven or eight years old.

Marcos started toward them, and Winston followed. Marcos spread his wings out full as he approached them and then he bowed low. The two angels with this small group bowed low, and there was quiet throughout the vast expanse for several minutes. The small group began to walk together with the angels guiding them and talking. They seemed to grow more excited as the minutes went by. Then the group stopped and looked back as if they were expecting others to follow.

Winston stepped up beside Marcos. First, he looked at the small group and then back up at Marcos. "What just happened? Who are those people that everything stopped? I mean, it is like you all have a schedule to keep, and there are tens of thousands, and this group stops the whole shebang."

"Those are martyrs. They were in a small church worshipping when followers of the prophet of the desert broke in and took them hostage. They drug them out of the church into the street. They were given the opportunity to renounce the Son of God and give allegiance to the prophet or die. The first man was the pastor of the church. He refused and began to pray in the Saviors name. They forced him to his knees and cut his throat and finally cut off his head. Then they turned to his wife. She refused to accept the prophet. Her son was brought in front of her. The crowd went wild. She was given another opportunity, but she refused and told her son to be strong. A group of men stepped forward and hacked them to death. Then a church member was forced to his knees and told to convert or die. He refused and was immediately killed. They have paid with their lives and now have a special place reserved for them until the end of it all."[5]

As they stood there, another man and woman appeared in the distance. They looked like they belonged with the first group. They stopped and stood there, separated from the first group. In a few moments, there were three more, two men and a woman. They did not move but stood looking toward the others. Finally, the pastor left the first group and started walking toward the others who had not approached. The one woman turned away and began to weep. The pastor spent time talking to each of them.

After a few moments he returned to the first group, and they continued their journey. Winston watched the five who remained behind. Marcos was busy, so he walked over to the group of five. As he approached, they looked up, and their faces were filled with defeat.

"What happened?" There was no tact in his question. He was curious. The others were martyrs and were already receiving praise. These were all alone, and the sadness was apparent.

One woman looked up and shook her head. Then a second woman spoke as the men lowered their heads.

"We have had to move twice in the last five years. As followers of the Lord, we were often attacked by the followers of the prophet. We have seen people beheaded, burned, drowned and beaten to death. Tonight, we were gathered in a small house church for prayer and study of the Word of God. The door exploded, and we found ourselves surrounded by over 100 followers of the prophet. Then One at a time they gave us the same choice to save our lives. They brought us out and told us to renounce our Lord and declare our allegiance to the prophet. They brought out a father first. There in front of his wife and child, he said no. They pushed him to the ground and cut his throat. Then they brought his wife and gave her the same choice. She refused, and she was also murdered in front of us all and her eight-year-old son. They brought the boy out and beat him before telling him to declare himself a follower of the prophet. He refused, and they killed him. Two more died. They kneeled and prayed as their throats were cut. It was chaos. I was so afraid of dying."

"Those were the five we saw first?" Winston asked her.

"Yes. Then my husband was taken out. He was trembling and standing in the blood of the others. I heard him call on the name of the prophet and the crowd went wild. They were cheering. My husband stood there while they were slapping him on the back. Next, the others did the same. I was the last one to be dragged before them. I looked at my dead friends and the ones who were alive. I did not want to die, so I spoke the prophets name. I heard the crowd cheering, and I thought I was safe."

She stopped talking and looked at the others. They all looked at each other.

She continued. "Then the leader of the group that took us. Shouted, KILL THEM! They are liars, and they only did it to save their lives. The crowd surged toward us. They had knives, and in the next moment, we found ourselves here. We all know what it says in the Word. We are judged not only on the confession of our faith but in how we finish our lives. If a righteous man or woman turns from their righteousness, they will die.[6] The Lord was clear that if we deny Him before men, he will deny us before the Father who is in heaven.[7]" She stopped talking. She looked at the others, and they started walking slowly onward. This small group came so close to obtaining eternal life and yet missed with the greatest sin possible. They had denied the Lord himself when it absolutely mattered the most.

As they moved on, Marcos returned from the front of the line. He was looking toward the ones who had come first. He pointed, "They are the true saints of God." Marcos' words spoke with awe and respect that comes from serving in a place where the majority of those who arrive were unprepared to face the end of life.

Winston looked at Marcos looking at the second group. "You mean, they came within a breath of eternal life and blew it?"

"It goes both ways. The day the Lamb died on the cross there was a man who asked to be here with the Lord forever. With only moments to live he was accepted and granted eternal life. He had been a thief and was sentenced to death, but because he repented with his last breath, he was granted entrance. He had nothing to offer but his faith, and it was accepted. You should have seen his arrival. Everyone was so torn as we heard of the sacrifice of our Lord for all who would believe. Then in an instant, the Lord had arrived a short time before, the thief who called on the Lord to save him was the first one to arrive who had declared his faith in the Master. The guy on the other side who denied Him while mockingly calling out "Are You not the Christ? Save Yourself and us!" arrived here almost at the same time. What a contrast as the two thieves stood in the lines. The one had mocked the Master beside him on the cross and then showed up here to face Him as his judge. While the other one was the first one to receive the Lamb as his Savior."

"So, what happens to the martyrs now?"

"Come, I will show you and deal with that woman we sent to the front of the line. I want her out of there before they arrive. They will need time to adjust to all that has happened. They will be guided toward the front of the line. They will be shielded from seeing those who had turned away and called the false prophet's name. It is only about rewards for them now. Their sorrow is gone."

Marcos spread his wings and took off. Winston found himself following close behind. There was a sense of motion and direction but not of height or a fear of falling. It was as if that did not matter here. Winston looked as lines came in and stretched across the expanse. Some were full, and some were almost empty and were disappearing as there was no one to walk on them. Even as this happened new lines appeared, and people started walking down them. As he looked around, he marveled at the simplicity of the place. How each line came in and moved toward the great doors at the far end. Each person on each line would have their time before the Master who is the Lamb

THE FRONT OF THE LINE

"For not even the Father judges anyone, but He has given all judgment to the Son, so that all will honor the Son even as they honor the Father. He who does not honor the Son does not honor the Father who sent Him., John 5.22-23

Winston and Marcos descended toward the place where all the lines seemed to end. There was a large double door that reached up a great distance and which appeared to be massive. On the two doors were the symbols for the Omega and the Alpha. The Omega was on the left door, and the Alpha was on the right door, it was the opposite of the way it usually appears. The woman and the two red angels were at the front of the line waiting on Marcos and Winston. They were still holding on to her arms but had put her down. Marcos approached them and signaled for them to step back away from her.

"Now, you wanted to talk to the one who is in charge, and I am going to make that opportunity happen for you. You are about to discover that you have wasted your life and are not ready to be here. That is an observation on my part that will either be proved or disproved in a short time." As he spoke, the large doors started to open. It showed a large hallway that was rounded at the top and looked like it was lined with black marble and stretched for a distance of over 400 meters. There was one small red line in the center of the hall on the floor starting at the door and running its length.

"Go on. This is what you wanted." Marcos pointed

toward the door almost as if to say; this cannot happen fast enough.

The woman stood looking at the doors as they swung completely open. Then she defiantly turned and started walking. She stopped at the doors and turned around.

"Why is the omega first and the alpha second? That does not seem to be right. I thought she was the alpha and the omega, the beginning and the end." She stood there looking at Marcos waiting for an answer.

"HE," Marcos emphasized HE clearly and distinctly, "is the Alpha and the Omega." He responded with a defiant voice that echoed disdain and power at the same time. "But that is on the doors for all who pass through, and it is about your life. This is the omega of your former life. It ends here. When you die, the next event is Judgment.[8] The few moments you spend here in these lines are to help you adjust while you are suspended between earth and eternity. All the decisions of your life are now tallied up, and you have nothing left but to hear your fate. That is why the end or omega is followed by the alpha. Your eternal existence is now about to start. For you, this is the end and the beginning. Now you need to go down the hall and face the real Alpha and the Omega, and I might add, you are about to discover that you will not be speaking to any so-called precious Mother Sophia."

The woman stood motionless. Something had suddenly changed. It may have been that she was aware this was real, or it may have been the realization that she was totally wrong, and it was going to cost her. "What if I don't want to go down that hall? Who is going to make me?" She recovered her attitude of defiance. She took several steps away from the doors back toward Marcos.

Marcos nodded his head, and the angels moved forward and instead of grabbing her they both drew flaming swords and began herding her down the hall with the blazing tips. On several occasions, she cried out in pain as they jabbed her. She began to rapidly move down the hall, followed by the two red angels with their swords right behind her. The doors started to close, and the three disappeared into the darkness. Winston watched until the doors closed again.

"What happens to her now?" Winston was deeply concerned as he saw his fate unfolding before him. He had gone from the back of the line to the front and now realized that this could well be the worst place in all of eternity to be if you were not ready.

"Come I will show you what you are allowed to see." They began to rise and move toward the side of the two large doors. As they did a small entrance opened on the side about halfway up. It was not a door, but an opening that appeared as the wall seemed to melt away into a mist. The door was about eight feet tall and wide enough for Marcos and Winston to enter side by side. The top of the doorway was rounded, and there was suddenly a sweet smell of flowers and spices that penetrated their nose, mouth, and eyes. This hall was bright white and looked to be as long as the other one below where the woman had gone. They moved down it without speaking. As they approached the end, there was a crystal-clear wall that rose up and showed a massive chamber or room. Winston moved toward the transparent wall, and as he looked in, he saw the woman and the two red angels below. They were tiny and about halfway across the room. The woman was shaking her fist and screaming at the two angels guarding her as she was herded toward a black square about halfway toward the front. The room was white, whiter than anything Winston had ever seen before. At the far end, there was a great white seat in the front center of the room with seven giant lampstands on all sides. These were ablaze with light even as there was no flame. The light from them hung above the lampstands and glowed filling the room with their light. Their great light was overshadowed by an even greater light coming from the throne.

The woman was pushed forward by the angels until she stopped on the center of the large black marble platform. As she did, the angels pulled back and bowed their heads and fell to their knees. Winston had so focused on the woman and the angels he did not see that the white throne was occupied. He did not know if the person had always been there or had suddenly appeared. He felt the room where he was shaking and looked as Marcos bowed his head and fell to his knees. Winston felt the voice vibrations rush through his body as it spoke to the woman. It was the sound of the ocean as it beats against the shore with huge waves. It was the sound of rushing water in a mountain stream. It was the sound of rain falling through the trees.[9] It was everywhere and at the same time refreshing, and it was terrifying.

The woman's demeanor had changed, and she sank to her knees in the center of the large black marble block. Her head was down. She was no longer fighting. The moment had come, and she was now before the real Alpha and Omega. It appeared she was shaking as if crying uncontrollably.

Instantly Winston knew who this was on the great white seat and what was happening. This was the Son of God. He was exactly as John had seen him. He was wearing a long white robe, and there was a golden sash around his chest. His hair was white like pure wool, and his eyes burned like flames from the hottest fire. He was standing, and his feet looked as if they were a metal bar heated in the hottest blast furnace.[10] When Winston tried to look at his face, it was like looking into the sun on the brightest and hottest day of the year. Winston fell to his knees and for a moment bowed his head and closed his eyes. Then he whispered, "Praise God, the Lord Almighty."[11]

How long his eyes were closed he did not know. He was afraid to open them at first. He was not the one being judged here, but it was a foreshadowing of what he could expect. Marcos touched him on the shoulder, and when Winston looked, he saw the angel was standing and looking toward the room.

"That woman has officially faced the Lord God Himself and has seen the truth. She will not speak here; there is nothing for her to say." There was movement in the room far below, and even over the vast distance, Winston could see what was happening. Halfway between the throne and the woman was a being. He could not be clearly seen or described, but He was there all the same.

"That is the Holy Spirit. He is both the defense counsel and the prosecution here. It is his duty to convict this woman of either being a follower of the Lord or to convict her of rejecting the Lord in her life."[12] He is only allowed to speak the truth and as such is the only one who will speak here today about the life of this woman." As Marcos spoke there rose before the woman a pedestal that had a great book on it. It was as no book Winston had ever seen. Its pages turned as it rose and when the pages stopped turning the Holy Spirit approached and looked. The page was empty. The Holy Spirit closed the book and turned toward the throne with his back to the woman.

"What just happened? What was that book anyway?"

"That, Mr. Winston Cummings was the Lamb's Book of Life.[13] If your name is not in that book, you don't get in. There are no exceptions."

"How do you get your name in there?" Winston spoke even before he thought.

"You have Bibles in your house. You have a wife who believes. You have been to church numerous times, and you don't know. Shame on you. The Holy Spirit convicts a person because they do not believe in the Son of God.[14] When a person believes and repents of their sinful life, their name is entered into the book with the blood of the Lamb of God that was shed on Calvary. Like the blood was passed over when the Hebrews were freed from Egypt, so each person who applies His blood to their lives will have their sins forgiven and have their names put in the Lambs Book of Life." Marcos was preaching. Winston was listening. He had heard this before. His pastor last Easter had preached this very message. There was motion in the room. The woman was now lying flat on her face, and the angels had pulled way back, the book was gone. The black floor beneath her was now glowing red and looked like a square lake of molten lava. She sat upright and jumped to her feet. As she did, she suddenly began to drop through the floor into a river of fire and in a moment, she was gone. The floor returned to the black marble shape and lowered back down. Winston stayed there on his knees. He was stunned. He was again questioning the reality of what was happening.

Below a woman walked into the room. She was elderly, but as she crossed the room, she was changed. She was revived and grew younger. She went to the center of the square, and it lifted. She fell to her knees and raised her hands in the air. She did not hide her eyes as the other woman did. She was worshiping God at her own judgment. The process was repeated but this time when the book was opened her name was there. Two angels approached her and lifted her to her feet. They placed a white robe on her, and the three walked toward the side of the room together. A door opened, and for a moment Winston saw a blue light shining. She stepped into the light, and the door went shut. Where it had been was completely smooth.

Marcos was in no hurry and Winston could not bring himself to look away. The process this time was very different than the others. A procession of angels entered the room and formed a line on either side with a path between them that lead to the black platform. There were thousands of them on either side. As Winston watched a dark-skinned man, who looked to be about fifty entered the room. Marcos spoke.

"This one arrived a short time before you did. He was a pastor of a church in Africa. Last night heathens came claiming to represent their prophet. They burned the church and took the pastor out in the street and made everyone come out to watch. Then they gave him a chance to recant his beliefs and pray to the prophet. He refused, so they killed his son. Then they killed his two daughters in front of him. They brought his wife and abused her before killing her. He prayed for strength and power. He prayed those who were doing this could discover the forgiveness for their sins. They told him all he had to do was deny Jesus and spit on the cross they gave him. He refused even with all he had seen and all the pain in his heart at losing his family he would not turn away from his Lord and Savior. Then they killed him by roasting him in a fire pit for hours. His son, daughters, and wife all died believing. They passed through here yesterday and are gathered with the other martyrs under the throne at the center of eternity. Right before this man died, he cried out, "JESUS INTO YOUR HANDS I COMMIT MY ETERNAL SOUL." This is how heaven greets those who die for Jesus. There is a greater crowd gathered on the other side. When he arrives, all heaven will cheer. Those martyrs you saw arriving will all come here and be received this way. They have faced the fear of death and remained true. This is a time when more are dying for their faith than in all of history. This is repeated daily from various locations around the world."

The book rose up and was opened, and his name was there. His robe was brought, and Winston felt the voice of the one on the throne shake the room. Marcos smiled and spoke the words for Winston to know what was being said.

"Well done my good and faithful servant, enter and share the joy of your Lord."[15]

Winston stayed there on his knees watching as each one entered the room and was judged. They were either ready or not ready. It was amazing to see how few had taken the time to prepare for eternity. Most of them had chosen some false god or path of enlightenment. The exit of the unrighteous was dramatic to watch. They always jumped to their feet trying to escape the coming end. Each time they were sucked down through the glowing floor and were gone. Winston did not ask about that right now. He was amazed and terrified at the same time. Those people had died on the same day he had and were now spending eternity paying for the choices in their lives. They had rejected the only way out of here. They had chosen the world, its riches, pleasures, and lies over the Lamb of God.

Winston watched as a man entered and walked up to the center of the judgment platform. He recognized him as one of several preachers he had met earlier. As he watched, things were different this time than many of the others.

"What is happening? Isn't that one a preacher? Shouldn't he be going right in?" Winston was watching trying to see what was happening. The Holy Spirit had not yet entered. The Lamb's book of life had not risen. The platform had not lifted as it had for the others, so they were on the same eye level with the Master on the great white throne of judgment.

Marcos looked toward Winston and then back into the room. "Everyone who enters gives an account. The first question is about whether the blood of the Lamb has been called on for forgiveness. If it hasn't, then the matter is closed, and it becomes eternal judgment a person is facing. If the blood has been applied, then comes the question of faithfulness."

Winston interrupted Marcos. "Wait, there is more to it than just getting saved. I know I heard preachers say all you have to do is accept Jesus and have your sins forgiven."

"Winston, the Lord was clear when he was on earth that it takes more than some spoken words. It takes a life of service. Do you remember the parable of the ten virgins? Five were wise, and five were foolish. Five were ready for the master's return, and five were not.

When the master returned and found the five who were ready, they were taken into the feast, and the door was shut. The others could not get in and were turned away by the master himself. They came to the door and cried, "Lord, Lord, open to us." But he answered, 'Truly I say to you, I do not know you." That is not a cute story. It is how the Lord made it plain that he expects and rewards the faithful. Remember the ten we saw earlier, how five of them were ready, and five made the wrong choice and were not prepared? Everyone still is held accountable for their life and service to Him.

It is even tougher for preachers and teachers of the Gospel. James, the brother of the Lord, wrote about this as a warning and as a promise. He wrote, 'Let not many of you become teachers, my brethren, knowing that such a person will incur a stricter judgment.'[16] Preachers and teachers of the Gospel are responsible for their lives and for what they teach."

"Wait a minute. Are you telling me preachers are responsible to God for what they preach?"

"It goes even deeper than that. They are responsible for the results if they have not preached or taught the truth if they have misled or spoken falsely. They are responsible if they contradict the Master Himself."

"I don't understand."

"They are on two levels. There are those who you could call false prophets or false teachers. They teach heresies, and some even deny the master himself. Their judgment here will be swift.[17] There is the second group; they are believers, but they have changed the message. Some were believing they are helping people and the message in the Bible is too harsh. They teach that Jesus is Love and will not punish anyone even though he said exactly the opposite. He was plain when he said, "Truly, truly, I say to you, he who hears My word and believes Him who sent Me, has eternal life, and does not come into judgment, but has passed out of death into life."[18] By teaching false doctrines or contradicting the Lord Himself they are bringing judgment on themselves by what they have preached.

The Master said he would send his angels and they 'would gather out of His kingdom all stumbling blocks, and those who commit lawlessness, and will throw them into the furnace of fire, in that place, there will be weeping and gnashing of teeth.'[19] Some of those stumbling blocks are preachers and teachers, and when they get here, they are greatly surprised. They often can preach about the world going to hell but forget 'The LORD will judge his people'[20] too.

Just last week a preacher of fame whose name you would know came here. He walked with confidence up to that platform and was sure his name was in the book of life, but it wasn't. He was shocked. That stricter judgment came into play. This preacher had written a book claiming he knew when the end of time was. That he had figured it out from some secret code, remember the Lamb said Himself, 'But of that day or hour no one knows, not even the angels in heaven, not the Son, but the Father alone.[21] Here was a preacher of the gospel of truth contradicting the Son. He had the truth of the Kingdom all messed up. His confidence melted away on that platform. Imagine you are facing the creator Himself and he asks you a question. 'Who is right you or me? I said only the Father knows and you said you know too. So, who is right, you or me?'

"What happened?' I mean if you are facing God and he asks you a question like that?"

"He was on his knees when he said, 'You are Lord.' The truth is in you and you alone. I was wrong. Please forgive me."

That preacher was one of many I have seen come through here who thought they were smarter than God. Some of these preachers denying clearly defined sins and calling them alternative lifestyles, taking it upon themselves to redefine sin and reject the Word of God. While other preachers are wanting the world to know they have new knowledge about the Kingdom of God and have discovered unknown secrets in the Word of God. In each case, they face the God who set the rules and whose precious Word of God they have ignored. He does not take that lightly. They face a greater judgment. Many do not make it.

Winston looked back toward the room and saw it filling up with angels again. They were standing all around and floating in the air. Winston stepped closer to the edge and looked toward the entrance. There was Nancy in her wheelchair coming into view. Her angel was pushing her as she entered the room. At the edge of the marble platform, they stopped, and the angel walked around in front of her. He bent down and whispered into her ear and then stepped back and offered her his hand. She took it and the little girl who had never taken a step or stood up before leaned forward and rose up onto new legs. She was transformed before them all. Suddenly she was a beautiful young woman standing there holding the arm of an angel. She spun around and twirled on her toes. Bending down she ran her hands up and down her legs and then stood up straight. Stepping forward she walked to the center of the platform and bowed down. Even as she rose back up her clothes changed again, and they became a light blue ballet dress. She began to dance, spinning on her toes and pointing her hands in the air as she gracefully used her new legs to perform. The room was transfixed as her motion carried her up above the platform. She slowed down and settled down onto the platform again. She slowly turned around, and the room exploded in applause. Tears were rolling down her face as she finally stopped and again bowed before the throne. The book was opened, and her name was there as everyone expected.

She stepped down off the platform and touched her wheelchair as it faded from existence. She moved forward to the throne. As she did, the One on it changed and reached out to meet her with a hug. He was not only her Lord and Savior he was also her friend and defender.[22]

The angel came forward with a white robe and placed it around her shoulders, and the two walked toward the door that had again opened, and they disappeared into the blue light.

Winston walked over to Marcos. "Does that happen often?"

"Well, actually, yes it does happen almost every day. Many come into the court who have endured and who discover that eternity will be all their dreams come true and so much more. Nancy has always wanted to dance. She loved the ballet and has prayed over and over to be allowed to perform at least once. The master wanted to share this moment with her, so he made it part of her celebration of arrival and acceptance."

Marcos spoke, the room cleared out, and others came and went. Then the Chinese pastor from earlier entered the chamber. Even before he made the platform, he had bowed low and had to be helped up by the angel. The pastor was crying and holding his hands over his eyes as he stood there. His whole body began to shake, and then he raised his arms over his head and shouted, "YES! YES! PRAISE GOD, YES!" He bowed down and became motionless except for the sobbing of joy that shook his body over and over.

Then he moved forward receiving his robe and was escorted to the entrance and into the blue light. Next Reverend Capps walked in and strutted forward toward the platform as if he owned the place. Even as he did an angel stepped in front of him and stopped him. Reverend Capps was a little shocked, and it was then that what was happening must have hit him. He had been so busy telling everyone about his accomplishments that he had not been paying attention to where he was and what was happening. The angel stepped aside, and it was then the pastor saw the throne and the One who sat on it. He stood there staring, overcome by everything that was happening. The angel motioned Reverend Capps toward the platform. He stepped up on the platform. "Reverend Capps here Lord. I have been very busy for you. I have preached messages for the last forty years. Raised money for missions to build schools. I have fought against smoking, drinking, drugs, dancing, sexual perversions of various kinds. I have lead rallies where hundreds joined the local church. Lord…"

Suddenly the one on the throne spoke, and the room shook. Rev. Capps backed up and fell on his face. He had seen himself and his preaching as so important. "'I never knew you; DEPART FROM ME, YOU WHO PRACTICE LAWLESSNESS.[23] You were never my servant. You spent your life drawing attention to yourself and claiming to do it in my name.

People have rejected me because of your self-righteousness."

Reverend Capps lifted his head and spoke, in the vast room it was clear and distinct. "But Lord, I have preached for the last forty years. I have lead hundreds, maybe even thousands, to you. I have taught lessons from the Word in ten different countries. I have three degrees and have written three books to help students understand Greek. I have stood against all sorts of sins and have never smoked, drank or cursed." He stopped, satisfied that he had done enough to earn his spot here.

"No, that was about you, not me. You have built your eternal life on what you were able to do. Without the blood, your actions are a life built on sand. I don't care how many joined your church or how many degrees you have. A man's pride will bring him low,[24] and yours will bring you as low as they go." The sound of his voice echoed as he finished speaking.

The silence was absolute when he finished. Then the Master leaned forward and spoke in a soft voice. "You have earned nothing with your preaching or teaching or your degrees. You have not lived as my servant but as if you were the one who was important. You may have pointed people to me, but you did it all so they would applaud your life and your success. It was my blood that was shed, and your education and accomplishments are nothing. I never knew you. Away from me."[25] At that moment the floor changed, and the pastor sunk into it and was gone in an instant.

Winston was shocked. He looked at Marcos. "Wait a minute. That guy was a pastor, and he did not make it. How is anyone going to get in?"

"Winston, haven't you been paying attention? It is about Him in your life. The people you have met today come in two types. There are those who serve him and those who don't. It is about accepting what he has done for you and then what you do with it. When the angels appeared to the shepherds, they told them, "Today in the town of David a Savior has been born to you; he is Christ the Lord." That is everything you need to know. First, he is Savior. He gave his life to pay for the sins of all who will accept this gift. Second, he is the Christ or the deliverer and protector. He wants to be involved in every part of your life. He was there with the Chinese pastor in prison, giving him strength in those difficult times. Finally, he must be the Lord of your life. This is so hard, and so many want the first two without being willing to submit to the third. The choice is to accept his gift of forgiveness, protection, and bow and serve Him with your life and be rewarded here. If you don't make Him your Lord, you are fooling yourself. The pastor thought he was essential and did not make Him Lord of his life. He was the lord of his own life and believed God would pay him for all he did instead of serving Him for all he had received and did not deserve.

Here 'every knee will bow, and every tongue will confess,'[26] but only those who served Him before they arrived will be rewarded with eternal life. All others receive eternal punishment. You have seen what just a few have seen who have not passed through this portal to eternity."

"But I thought he was love. How can he send anyone away to eternal punishment? I mean." He was not able to finish before Marcos interrupted.

"No, he does not decide. You do that before you get here. He merely honors your choice. Either you are ready, or you are not. He waits right up to the last moment. I have seen individuals call on Him at the last moments of their life, and He has accepted them." Marcos turned and started back down the path to the room where all the paths converge at the doors.

"It is time for us to go. I have matters to attend to. You have seen what happens. If you stay here, I hope you are ready. If you don't and get another opportunity, then you better make the most of it." Winston was still looking toward the court and saw the door open and the angels all applauding about something.

"Wait, did that preacher really not make it?"

Winston was stunned. Hey, if a preacher can be in trouble here what chance did he stand. It was apparent Marcos was not going to discuss it further as he was walking away.

Then Winston hurried down the hall to catch up with his guide.

"Hey, Marcos, what is happening? You know, back on earth. Am I dead or alive, coming or going? Am I staying here or going back?"

"When I know you will know. Till then I have work to do, and you need to stay close."

They were now walking down a path that looked out into darkness on all sides. There were two ribbons of light up ahead. One glowed orange, the other blue. They seemed to dance in the darkness, but they lit up nothing except themselves. They went off in opposite directions. Winston followed Marcos without saying a word. He was trying to put it all together, but it was tough to comprehend.

THE VIEWING PLATFORM

"Then they will go away to eternal punishment, but the righteous to eternal life." Matthew 25.36

Marcos was walking briskly into the darkness and Winston felt he was sprinting to catch up. It was total blackness except for the two ribbons of light and a dim light around Marcos. The angel stopped watching the ribbons. The one that went off toward their right glowed red and orange. It whipped around and in the great distance seemed to separate several times. Each ribbon whipped off into the distance. It was apparent that they flowed almost like a river's current away from where they were standing and toward faintly lit areas in the far distance. The one on the left was different. It was a single light glowing blue ribbon. It did not whip as the red one did but smoothly flowed in gentle curves. There in the distance was a bright light surrounded by darkness. The light went out, but it appeared there was nothing to reflect it, so it vanished into the darkness.

Winston spoke first in a low voice. He had an idea what it was but was not sure. "What are those?" He was not even sure what to ask or how to ask the question.

"Those are the ribbons of judgment. That one." He pointed to the red and orange one. "Leads to eternal punishment.[27] It is where the eternal fire burns.[28] That is a place filled with weeping and gnashing of teeth.[29] "Their worm does not die, and the fire is not quenched."[30] It was prepared especially for the devil and all his followers.[31] It flows away from here and to the 'Lake of Fire'[32] where they will be forever and ever.

He never wanted that one, but it is the only way an impartial God can deal with sin and sinfulness. The Devil is a liar. He told the first lie.[33] He continues to lie. He says a loving God would not send anyone to hell, but the truth is where you humans end up is your choice, and God always honors your choice."

"Wait, I would never choose to go to hell, yet if I hear you right, I may end up there."

Marcos stood watching the two ribbons as he responded to Winston. "But it is more than a choice; it is what is deserved unless you respond to God. People are full of excuses. They want to believe there is no such thing as sin. If it doesn't exist, then they are fine. People don't start out as sinners, but they all do it. All have sinned[34] and are without excuse. Most people don't think about it, but everything in the world points to Him, so people are without any excuse.[35] People don't think about the consequences of sin and rejecting God.[36] That is what this is all about here. The good news is God saw all of this and made a way out for anyone who wants to take it. He sent his Son to die in your place.[37] That is how much he loved all of you. Then it comes down to your acceptance or rejection of Him. This is both external and internal. You have to believe in your heart and confess or live for Him.[38]"

Marcos stopped talking for a moment. Winston stood looking out toward the two ribbons as they twisted in opposite directions from each other into the darkness.

"The other one." Marcos pointed toward the blue one. "It leads to eternal life and the eternal throne of God."

"Wait I thought that was the throne of God we just

saw."

"That was the great white throne of judgment. [39] It is not located in the third heaven because it would make God a liar if it were. God has said about heaven 'Nothing impure will ever enter it, nor will anyone who does what is shameful or deceitful, but only those whose names are written in the Lamb's book of life.'[40] You have to come through here to get there."

Winston looked at Marcos and knew the angel was wrong. He thought it thru before he spoke. "What about that angel that rebelled against God and the bunch of them got kicked out? The one who became the devil, you know, Lucifer." Winston felt pretty good for remembering that one. He had not been asleep when that lesson was taught. Everyone knew that was true. That proved the angel wrong and, if he was wrong there his chances might be better than he had thought.

Marcos turned sharply toward Winston and shook his head in disapproval and disagreement. "Lucifer is not the devil." He was firm with his answer. "Lucifer means morning light and is only found in one place in the Word of God.[41] He was the king of Babylon who was so arrogant he compared himself to God. Which any sane person would know is not what one should do. So, the king, also known as Lucifer was defeated. He was killed by a sword, and his body was not even buried but was trampled underfoot.[42] He rose up and placed himself in a position of power so great on earth he was described as being cast out of heaven when he died.[43] I was here the day he arrived. His arrogance would make that woman we saw earlier seem like nothing. He arrived and started marching down the aisle knocking people out of his way. He was the great king of the morning, the ruler of what he called heaven and earth. He thought his earthly kingdom extended even to heaven and made him something important. He marched right up to the doors of the Crown Court and started pounding. I don't think he paid attention to where he was for some time. When he arrived at the doors, he turned and started to walk back, but was met by twenty-four of the guards of order and justice. Those red fellows you saw earlier with their swords pulled. They surrounded him and marched him into the chamber. He said the same thing the bus driver said when she hit you, "Oh, God, NO!"

I was there that day. Rarely does He speak with anger but on that day He spoke, no He shouted at that man. "How dare you claim to represent, no, how dare you claim to be me! You puny worthless man! Even your sons will pay for your sins. They will be slaughtered.[44]"

The king was on his knees, weeping as most of them do. The closest he ever got to heaven and God was right here in the Crown Court of Judgment.

"NO, that is not the story I learned." Winston was confused.

Marcos continued, "Listen. In 1667 a blind poet who desperately needed money named Milton made his living making up a story that was published in ten separate booklets. The best way you could understand each booklet was like a weekly episode of your favorite television program. He knew just enough about the Bible to be dangerous. A verse here and a verse there. He was like the Old Man McDonald of the scriptures. Here a verse there a verse, everywhere a verse, verse. He cut and pasted them together until they made a great story. It became so popular that the devil, not Lucifer, but the real devil started using it himself. He liked the idea of almost taking God out and having been in heaven. Listen to me Winston James Cummings, no evil can enter heaven, and no evil can happen in heaven if it had happened once it could happen again. It did not happen, and it will never happen. If you make it to heaven, you will have made it to a place of eternal perfection. Eternally free from sin."

But I thought Lucifer was in heaven, I mean wasn't he cast down from heaven?" Winston was in his first real theological debate and was in way over his head. Far be it he had chosen the very judgment seat of God to have it, none the less he thought he was right.

"Winston." Marcos was smiling. "A little knowledge is a dangerous thing to put your trust in. Not that you will understand, but I will explain it anyway. There are three heavens written about in the Word of God. The first one mentioned is the one God created that holds the sun, moon and the stars. The one people look up at and marvel. That is the one you cannot see the end of. That is the first heaven. It has light that travels millions of years to arrive at earth that you call stars. Then the third heaven. It is the one that people leave here and get to spend eternity in. A couple of guys have come and gone back. John the disciple who wrote the book of Revelations tried his best to describe the place and failed miserably. The other was the apostle Paul. Now there was a guy who was awed and confused. Did not know if he was here in his body or whether he was floating around.[45] He saw and heard so much he got back, and all he could say about it was, awesome. He called the place, Paradise or the third heaven.[46] So heaven number one is the sky, and heaven number three is a short distance from here if you find your name in the Lambs Book of Life. Then we have guys like Lucifer the King of Babylon[47] believing he was so powerful and important that he begins to think he is God in heaven. That heaven is a place of power and authority. When he was defeated, it was described as falling from heaven or losing his power and authority. He was not in the first heaven which is the sky, and he was not in the heaven at the end of the blue ribbon. He was a sinner and sinners don't go there, and no one ever leaves there except the two I mentioned. Heaven one is the sky. Heaven two is a place that represents authority and power on earth, and Heaven number three is where the great eternal throne of God is at and where most people think they are headed until they get here and discover they never got their name into the Lamb's Book of Life." Marcos drew closer and looked down at Winston.

"Milton rode the red ribbon. He was so surprised when he got here, he was begging for a chance to go back and make it right. The number of people who have been misled by him I would hate to imagine what level he has sunk into. Ministers, theologians, politicians, ordinary people they all have been deceived. The Devil, Satan himself loves the story so much he keeps spreading it around. He liked the idea of being up in heaven and giving God a run for his money. But it never happened. Heaven is not now, will not be, and has never been a place where anyone sinned.

He is not the only one who has gotten it wrong. A few years ago, in your time on earth, a pastor wrote a book about coming to heaven and getting visited by angels. Had us walking around in bell bottoms and turtle necks, and no wings. His book was really popular but gave a lot of people false hope and led many away from the Lord. People were worshipping angels instead of the Master because of what he wrote. I was away in heaven when he came through, don't know what happened for sure but I have never bumped into him when I have been over there in the third heaven." Marcos turned and walked further up the dark corridor. Then he turned and came back.

"I don't understand. You have the Word of God given you by God so that you can spend eternity with Him. Yet, the majority of you either ignore Him or you make up your own ideas and then think God is going to let you in anyway. I wonder how many copies of the Word are located in your home? Have you ever read it?"

Winston did not speak. The angel had completely unloaded on him, taught him several lessons and questioned the sanity of the whole human race.

"Do you see that ribbon?" Marcos pointed at the red and yellow one. "That ribbon is a straight shot into eternal punishment. There is no way back. The people who enter the ribbon here will not arrive at the eternal lake of fire for tens of thousands of years. The eternal lake of fire is so far that the light fades into nothing and still there is space between us. See those black specks in the flow? They spark and twist around. They are the judged. They will never die, but they will always feel and never get relief. They have eternal bodies designed for eternity. God wanted them in heaven, but they chose not to accept His invitation or His terms." The ribbon twisted backward for a few seconds, and Winston could see the souls of those who were not ready but were flowing through the river of fire and justice away from them toward the vast darkness.

"How can a loving God send anyone to HELL?" Winston asked without thinking. He had heard it so many times that he blurted it out. "I did not think God would send anyone to hell. I don't understand how He can do that to anyone and still be seen as a loving and compassionate God."

"Let me ask you a better question. Why should an unbiassed God allow anyone who has sinned into heaven? Why would He want to do that anyway?" The angel was looking at Winston as he continued. "God did not do this to them. They choose their fate. Either by rejecting God in any number of ways or by ignoring him and denying his existence or his authority. God does not choose who gets their name in the book. You all do that for yourselves. Each person chooses to accept or reject his invitation.

God is a judge. Do you know what that means? God makes sure the proceedings are fair and impartial. That everyone gets what they deserve. It is about justice for the sinful and mercy for the faithful. It is pretty straight forward here. Any criminal coming into court hopes to get off on a technicality. Here, there are not any technicalities. No lies or excuses are accepted. There is none of the confusion of preexisting conditions and blaming others for what has happened. The soul that sins will die.[48] The one who sows to his own flesh will from the flesh reap corruption, but the one who sows to the Spirit will from the Spirit reap eternal life.[49] Those who accept the Savior are already justified. That is an old word which means they are found not guilty. Not because of what they have done but because of what He did for them. Then they are to live a righteous life. Which means they are to remain innocent by doing the right thing over and over, so when they get here, for them it is about rewards.

Remember, the Holy Spirit is the one who speaks the truth in the Crown Court. He is the attorney for everyone. No fancy excuses or psychological mumbo jumbo with competing experts. No blaming your father or mother because they did not give you enough hugs. If you have not taken care of getting your name in the Book of Life, you will not get into Heaven. There are no exceptions to that rule.

Those who do not accept God's grace or His free gift of forgiveness come here with a very different perspective on what is going to happen. They have been given every opportunity. They don't have any excuses when they get here, since the creation of the world His invisible attributes, His eternal power, and divine nature, have been clearly seen, being understood through what has been made, so that they are without excuse.[50] Many of them have removed Him from the equation by saying it is all some act of happenstance, thinking they crawled out of some primeval slime pool. They believe they exist because of happenstance and evolving steps and some random chance it all came together and, bang, it all came into being even while the very creation shows God's design in everything, he created.

Winston, I want you to imagine an alarm clock. You know one of the old wind-up kind with gears, screws, springs and such. Now imagine I take it apart and then put all the parts into a shoe box and tape it up. Then I give it to you and tell you to shake it up till it is an alarm clock again. How long would it take you to do that? Really, would you be willing to do that?" Marcos stopped. As he stood there surrounded by the darkness and the red cord of judgment whipped around in the void delivering souls to their eternal destination Winston puzzled the question.

"So, you will take it apart, and I am to shake it back together? If you gave me the necessary tools, I could not put it together. It would never be a clock again if all you were allowed to do is shake it to put it back together. Those people out there will arrive at their destination long before two pieces fit together. So, what is your point?"

"My point is, shaking that clock back together is equal to one step in the process you call evolution. Every step of every species would require you to shake a clock back together. That would be easier than any simple step in evolution. Look at all God created and how complicated it is. Humans are just beginning to see the depth of all He has done. Then they want to say a monkey is related to humans because of common design qualities. Of course, there are similarities. The Creator did not start over every time he made something. He used some of the very same designs and techniques throughout the creation. Part of that is to show there is a common Creator, but no...." He stopped for a moment and took a few steps away from Winston and then turned and continued. "No... they try and say it is all part of a chain of evolutional steps of random acts of chance. They show up here, and God will not put up with that. He has laid it out for them in so many different ways, and they still ignore him. It would take shaking billions or even trillions of clocks back together to equal what God did in all of creation. Man calls this evolution a series of random incidents that somehow evolve into intelligent life. They think if they can explain it without God that releases them from his power and authority."

"Come on. We have to go."

"Wait, I have another question. Really."

Marcos stopped and turned back. "OK, what is your question."

"I know it takes those in the red ribbon a long time to get where they are going. How long does it take those who walk through the door to eternal life to get there?"

"It is all but a moment, a twinkling of the eye. When the last person is judged, this place is being shut down and destroyed along with the old earth and all that man has touched. This place along with the eternal fire has been prepared for the devil and his angels.[51] He is not looking forward to this place any more than any of you are. When he gets here, he will be brought to the same platform, and he will bow and confess before facing his eternal punishment. That is why the demons asked to be put in the swine when He cast them out of the man by the lake.[52] Even the swine could not take it and ran into the lake and drowned." He started to walk again. "Come on I still have responsibilities to take care of. You will have to stay with me till everything is worked out about your situation."

THE JUSTICE SEAT OF GOD
SISTER ETHEL

We were not looking for praise from men, not from you or anyone else. 1 Thessalonians 2.6

They turned the corner to a hallway leading back toward the large area filled with the lines. As Winston looked back, he saw the darkness of the void, and for a brief moment the ribbon of red passed into his view and then was gone again. The hall he was in was not visible when in the viewing platform they had been on. They had been able to look in all directions, and all he could see was the two ribbons. He had been able to look beyond and yet now he was back in the vast area filled with lines. As he entered, he was now paying more attention to what was happening around him.

What had seemed like random lines were now beginning to resemble order. People were not being shuffled around. They were being put in categories and prepared to come before the final judgment in their lives.

They headed away from the doors of judgment and toward a line of people that had stopped. They were gathering together around a lady who was wearing a long flowing gown or robe that had many colors and beads on it. Some were watching, but several were waving their arms in the air, and two were on their knees bowing up and down before the woman.

All the lines were moving but this one. Marcos approached to within about thirty feet and stopped and looked back at Winston.

"Please wait here and do not wander off." I need to

deal with this, this…"

He appeared to be searching for words to describe the woman or the situation clearly, but he was finding it extremely difficult.

"Winston, I rarely am irritated, but for someone to arrive here and still think that there is any other God than the one they will face just beyond that door is wrong. To worship such a person here in this great chamber is the final sacrilegious action a person can take. I know it will make no difference in their final destination, but it still is repulsive to all of us who serve the one true God. We would never allow anyone to worship any of us and worship of this type is absolutely not going to continue on my watch.

When John the disciple was preparing to write the Book of Revelation, God brought him to Heaven. He made such a very grave mistake. He fell and started to worship the angel who had given him God's message. He was in Heaven bowing to an angel. It was wrong, but he was so overcome by all that was happening to him. The angel grabbed him and pulled him to his feet. He looked John right in the face and said, 'Do not do that. I am a fellow servant of yours and your brethren the prophets and of those who heed the words of this book. Worship God.[53]' We don't allow any worship here except if it is directed to God."

Winston looked at those bowing and the woman smiling at this event, and he realized that this was a huge mistake. He stopped and stepped back a little.

"I'll stay right here while you handle this situation."

Marcos turned and moved forward. Winston did not know how many angels suddenly appeared, but it was a significant number. How they had been summoned, he did not know, but one moment there was a small group worshiping the woman and the next moment the woman was alone as her followers were being carried away to other lines. Then Marcos approached the woman and pointed at her.

"You remind me of Jezebel in Revelations.[54] You allow people to worship you and you lead them astray with false prophecies and teachings. You have even taught them that to worship you is to worship God. I am going to take you to the front of this line where you are going to be next to be judged. I want you out of here." His voice was getting stronger and louder as he spoke. "You shall soon bow your knees to the one true God, and you shall confess who he is and who you are."

"Winston, I will send someone to stay with you till I can get back. I promise you as soon as we know something, we will let you know."

Marcos turned and grabbed the woman by her shoulders, and they were off toward the doors of judgment and the Crown Court.

Even as Marcos disappeared with the woman kicking and screaming a small angel approached Winston. This angel was shorter than most of them and was a pale grey. His wings were almost black except for the tips of them were white. He smiled and spoke softly.

"Well, I hear you are in limbo right now. That doesn't happen very often. You are the first one I have ever met who it has happened to. I must meet a lady who is almost here. I am Afriel. I think you will like this lady. She has quite a story."

He started off, and without thinking, Winston went along. He found himself smiling. He mused at the name Afriel and wondered if it had any meaning till he finally asked.

"What does your name mean?"

"Mean? It is not what it means. It describes who I am. I am the angel of youth. I got that name while on assignment on earth to a small child who named me. It stuck, and I like it."

"Ah, there she is." They had traveled a short distance back toward the grey mist, and a new walkway was forming as they approached. They slowed and watched as a very old lady emerged from the mist. It was one of only a few old person Winston had seen, and it was not until he saw her that he realized that fact.

Afriel spread his wings to get her attention and smiled at her.

"Ethel, it is so good to see you again."

"You! Well, it was not a dream I had." She smiled and looked at him with faded but delighted eyes.

"No, it was real. I know it was a tough time and I thought I was going to bring you back then. I have asked to be allowed to greet you and walk with you to the great hall." He extended his arm to escort her, and they began walking slowly.

"This is Winston. He is in limbo right now. He does not know if he is staying or leaving, coming or going. He has caused quite a stir."

She looked at him and spoke in an aged soft voice that almost cracked from sounding extremely tired.

"Well, at least you are here. I was almost here once, and then I wasn't. Came within a few heartbeats of getting here and then was called back."

Winston looked at Afriel with a question on his face but before he could speak Ethel spoke again.

"I thought this new body would be different. This one is old and broken like the one I left. I am not complaining now, but I was led to believe the new one would be better, perfect."

Afriel touched her hand softly and said, "Walk with me, and you will understand shortly, and I guarantee you will not be disappointed. Why don't you tell Winston your story? I know he will appreciate it."

"No, he is not interested in me."

"Oh, I think he is, and it will make the time pass while we walk. Go ahead and tell him."

"Where should I start? I don't know where to start."

"Let me help, and you can take over as we go along." Afriel was focused on taking care of Ethel. Winston thought he saw or heard or felt love. Not romantic love but a deep love of two friends who, though they had not seen each other for many years, were as if they had never been apart.

"All right then, where do you think I should start?"

"I think you should start with your home life."

"I haven't thought about that in forever."

"Please," Afriel called to her in a begging voice dragging the word out over several seconds.

"Silly Afriel, you make me laugh. You always made me laugh even when I did not know you were there."

"Winston, your name is Winston, right?" She looked toward him and spoke.

He nodded his head "yes" and smiled. Somehow it was wrong to speak if she was going to tell her story.

"Winston, I was raised on a farm by a very strict father. As a small girl, he was cruel to me. I think he wanted a son and never liked the thought of a daughter. When I was thirteen, my mother died, and shortly after that, he started taking advantage of me. It was a terrible life. It did not happen often, but when it did, I felt sick and hated myself for weeks at a time. I had no self-worth and lived in a daydream world most of the time. I wanted to escape but saw no way out. One Saturday when I was seventeen, I got to go on the train to the city to visit my aunt. I sat down on the train and rode looking out the window and wishing I could live anywhere but where I did. As I rode along, I looked down and there on the floor was a pamphlet from the Gospel Trumpet company. It was all about how much my heavenly father loved me and how he sent his Son to die for my sins. I remember it said He wanted to set me free. I started crying. I wanted to be free." She stopped and wiped a tear from her eye.

"I asked God to forgive me of my sins and to set me free. I went to my aunt's house and eventually told her about my life. She helped me, and I did not go back to my father."

They continued to walk, and her voice was a little stronger. The lines were filling in all around them, but the path they were on only had the three of them. Afriel's smile was wide, and his eyes were filled with affection as he looked at the old woman who was walking beside him.

"I got a job and started saving for the future. That is when I met a dashing man. He was ten years older than me, and he had a great job. He lived with his mother and cared for her. We fell in love and were married that same year. Things went well till one day he started feeling a little weak. By the weekend he was very sick and had to see the doctor. He had a rare blood disease and was so ill he couldn't return to work. He became bedridden and the responsibility of the family fell to me. His mother was now confined to a wheelchair and going blind. I cared for them while I worked ten hours a day for almost ten years." She stopped walking and looked around.

"This is really a fantastic place!"

"Go on. Winston needs to hear this, and I want to tell you a surprise when you get done. I have waited for most of your life to share it with you." Afriel held out his hand inviting her to start walking and talking. She stepped out slowly and continued.

"Then I got sick. I thought I was going to die. I wanted to die. I was rushed to the hospital. I had to leave my husband sick in bed and his mother in the wheelchair there. It was the first time in what seemed like forever I got to rest if you could call it that. I was so sick I remember I started walking up some stairs that went up and up. It was so beautiful, as I walked and I felt so good about going up them. Then I saw someone at the top holding out his hand to me. I wanted to grab that hand when I heard a voice calling my name. It was far away, but I could hear it calling. 'Ethel, Ethel, don't leave us. We need you.' I was going to go on up the steps, but then the voice called again. 'Ethel, please Ethel don't leave us.' I stopped and looked back, but when I looked up again, the steps faded. The person at the top pulled back his hand and was gone. Suddenly I woke up and was in a hospital bed. My blind mother-in-law setting beside me, crying and holding my hand begging me to come back. I started to cry. I did not want to be there. I got better and took care of them for several years. First, he died and then she did. I remember the feeling of sorrow for losing them and the relief from the burden of caring for them every hour I was not asleep or at work. I remember my two greatest joys were reading my Bible and going to church. I never missed church. I had made a commitment to the Lamb of God and made

Him the Master of my life. He had promised to set me free."

They stopped, and Ethel looked at her hands. Some of the wrinkles were gone. And she was standing a little more upright. She turned her hands over and over all the while smiling.

"Ah, so that is how it works."

"Ethel, please tell Winston what happened next. You know, when you got married again."

"I will Afriel. I am so enjoying this walk. I have not been able to walk like this for years. You know that."

He nodded his head, and she continued with her story.

"Well, after a couple of years I met a man. He was my age. His wife had died and, well, we fell in love and got married. It was fabulous. Walks in the park and plans for trips, I was not caring for anyone. Then it happened. It was like when you are experiencing something for the first time again. One day my husband started feeling ill. We took him to the doctor's office, and after some tests, we went in to get the results. I remember the doctor giving us the results. My husband had a rare blood disease. He had the same rare blood disease my first husband had. It was so rare most doctors never see one case. The chances of meeting two people who have it in your lifetime are so remote it is astronomical to think about, and I had married two men with the same extremely rare disease. I cared for him and worked full time for the next fifteen years. When he died, I was already physically broken and exhausted. My niece and her husband took me in. They provided for me for the rest of my life."

She stopped and smiled. "Look at me. I am standing straight for the first time in the last twenty years. I feel much better."

"Tell Winston what you did for the last thirty years. You could barely get around and spent most days in your tiny trailer in your niece's front yard."

"I wrote prayers and sent them to people who needed them. I wrote thousands of prayers, and when I was not writing prayers, I was praying for people. I kept a list of people to pray for. Every Sunday morning, Sunday night, Wednesday prayer meeting I listened to the prayer requests, and I prayed for them over and over till I knew they were answered. I love to pray, it was so easy and brought me so much joy. People started sending me prayer requests. People I did not know would call and ask for me to pray for them. I never once prayed out loud in a church service, but I guarantee I prayed for our pastors and their wives. I prayed when the enemy attacked them. I prayed for them and their children. I have known some great men of God, and I have seen how the enemy attacked them right in the church. I prayed for them because I could and because it brought me such joy. Do you know where I learned to pray?"

She addressed this question to Winston. He did not answer. It seemed to be a rhetorical question to him anyway.

"I learned to pray on the farm. I prayed to be free. Year after year I prayed to be free and finally God set me free. I prayed for my husbands and I prayed for my mother-in-law. I prayed for years. I learned the practice of prayer. I learned patience in prayer. I learned to pray whenever and wherever I was. I prayed and prayed. And, you know, I learned that God listened to my prayers. He liked my prayers. It was the one thing I could do even when I was on the farm. When I was married, and my husband was sick. When the second one got sick I already knew how to pray for him. When I got arthritis and was unable to do hardly anything else, I prayed. I love to pray. It is the gift God gave me. He trained me to pray. The devil wanted to stop me. He used my father to try and stop me and turn me away from God, but I focused on my Heavenly Father even before I knew all He had done for me. He used disease and sickness to try and break me, but I used it as an opportunity to focus on God. I know what he intended for evil God used for good.[55] It was my choice, and I chose God. I felt there was no other choice. He had done so much for me, and I was asked to do so little compared to His sacrifice. I was one of God's prayer warriors, and I bet the devil is glad I finally died. I prayed against him, and his forces and I beat down the gates of hell with my prayers every single day." Her voice had become forceful and sure.

They all stopped again. The lines on her face were almost gone. Her hands had grown younger, and she was standing upright. Her hair had changed from grey to an auburn. Her blue eyes sparkled.

"Afriel, This is so fantastic, I could not have ever imagined this would happen like this." She grabbed him and squeezed hard.

"The wings, careful of the wings. You are squeezing the wings."

She laughed. "Sorry I am just so full of joy."

She looked at Afriel and a tear-filled her eye. "Wait, it was you. You were the one waiting for me at the top of the stairs. That is why I recognize you. It is why you seem like an old friend. Tell me I am right."

"Yes, I was there. I was always there.

She looked at him, and her eyes narrowed, and her

brow furrowed as she thought about what he had said. "There is more isn't there. I feel there is more."

He stepped around in front of her. She was now much younger and looked him right in the eyes.

"I have always been there. I was assigned as your guardian angel when you were born. I was there at night when you cried out, and I cried out too. It hurt me to see him hurt you. I am so glad you looked down on the train and saw the gospel track that was there. I did everything I could to make sure you were alone, and no one interfered. It was not an accident it was there on the floor of the train that day. Wow, you should have seen how complicated it is to get a gospel tract from Anderson, Indiana, to the floor of that train for you to find in central Mississippi.

I was there when you married and when your husband became sick. I was watching over you and answering the prayers as God directed me. There were times I did not understand. I cannot see the future like He can and was unaware of his plans for you as a great prayer warrior. When you became sick, I asked to be allowed to guide you like I am doing today. I was so happy knowing you would be free and not suffer or be alone anymore. But you were never alone. You always had Him in your heart. I remember the look on your face when you were called back by your mother-in-law.

God had grand plans for you. I am so proud of you and how much you did with your life. You served Him as few others have. Your prayers covered thousands every week. The enemy hated to hear you were praying."

This time they hugged each other. The young woman smiled at her guardian angel and tears of joy ran down both of their faces. Even as they hugged

Marcos came floating in.

"All right, Afriel, I think it is time to get her inside. He is waiting for her. He knows she is coming. He wants to thank her and has a few special rewards lined up for her. He has invited you to come in with her and take her all the way. That doesn't happen often, but I know how important she has been to you."

"Thanks, I appreciate this opportunity. I feel so much better knowing she is here, safe and sound. I thought the enemy would never stop throwing stuff at her." Afriel offered her his arm one more time, and they started walking forward again. A beautiful young woman and the grey angel who had served as her guardian angel.

Marcos nodded his head and stepped back.

"Winston, I have not heard anything yet about what is happening to you so let's go. Afriel needs to get her inside, and you need to stay close to me. Today you got to see why we love doing what we do. We love serving the Master and helping get the message out through those we watch over."

THE LONG, LONG LINES

You judge by human standards; I pass judgment on no one. But if I do judge, my decisions are right, because I am not alone. I stand with the Father, who sent me. John 8.15-16

The lines which seemed random at first began to make a little sense as he watched the people pass by where he was standing. They all came in on one side of the great room and progressed toward the other side where they ended in four lines. As the lines of people moved across the room, he noticed that there were angels standing in the lines holding small bundles in their arms. Winston strained to see what they were holding and figure out why they were in line but could not get a good enough look to tell for sure.

Marcos was dealing with another person who did not have the grasp of what was happening to her. She was shaking uncontrollably and refusing to go forward. The line was passing by her. As they approached, she was begging the angel.

"Please let me go back. I must tell my children one more time. I want them to be ready. PLEASE...." Her voice trailed off, and she softly asked again, "Please..."

A blue angel was standing with his arm around her, and she turned and buried her head in his chest as she sobbed. "I have prayed for them every day. I only want one more opportunity to talk to them."

Marcos nodded to the angel, and he started walking forward, helping the woman. She finally got back in line, and whatever the angel said to her, she began to smile and moved on.

Several angels gathered around with Winston as Marcos helped the woman move forward. Winston asked, "will she be alright?"

An angel with yellow wings and a white robe responded. "Oh, yes. That happens from time to time. She will be ushered into heaven, and the memories of lost loved ones will be gone. Our Lord will not want any sadness or sorrow in heaven."

I remember when Anjeze Bojaxau came. She was such a different person. She did not want to go to the judgment court but wanted to stay here and help everyone adjust. She started trying to help comfort people. She was going from line to line trying to help those who did not understand. It took forever to get her to go forward." The angel looked at Winston. "Oh, sorry you don't know her by that name. She was known as Mother Teresa. She spent her life working to help those with HIV, leprosy, tuberculosis. She was a remarkable woman. She was strongly opposed to abortion and believed in the sanctity of human life as a gift from God. She was a real servant and wanted to stay here and help."

"So did God allow that?" It was Winston asking the question. Here he was standing around with a group of angels listening to them tell stories about those who came here. Some ready but most were not.

"No, this was not where she was needed. She went on and is working with babies who were aborted. They come here and have a lot of adjusting. They never had a real life to prepare them for here, so it is much more difficult for them. Sister Anjeze that is what she likes to be called now helps them. She loves her work but wishes it was not necessary."

"Who is the most interesting person you have ever met while doing this?" Winston was getting into the conservation and had lost focus on why he was here and that he did not know his own outcome.

A cream-colored angel smiled. "We all have our stories. When we get started, it is hard to get us stopped. Me, personally, well it was when Abraham got here. I was on my first assignment and was so excited. I got almost everything wrong. I forgot the protocols and had lines running in reverse and even had one line going in a big circle. Those people were never going to get anywhere. They would walk by and see the doors leading to eternity and go back around. What is even worse is no one caught on for over a week. It is one of the all-time greatest mess ups in this whole place. Anyway, Abraham shows up, and when he got here, he fell to his knees. Right over there, just inside the mist and began to cry. Everything stopped; I mean everything. The lines, the angels flying, the judgment doors were open, but no one went in. It was Marcos who approached him. When Abraham saw him, he jumped up and hugged him like he was an old friend. It was Marcos who was one of the three angels who visited Abraham and told him about the promise of an heir. That was when Sarah laughed and did not believe.[56] He was there with the Spirit of God. Abraham was so pleased to see Marcos they must have hugged and laughed for what seemed like forever."

"Why was he crying."

"Joy, sheer joy. He had lived his whole life in tents believing there was something greater. He had wandered believing a promise spoken to him by strangers from heaven. There were many who doubted. He spent his whole life looking for the city which has foundations, whose architect and builder is God.[57] He dragged his family around in tents following a vision given to him by God. He taught it to them. He told them the stories over and over. He would sit by the fire, and his eyes would light up as he described the feeling of speaking directly to a messenger sent from God. So, when he got here, he thought this was heaven and was so glad he sat down and cried. Marcos had to work to get him to go the rest of the way. Abraham kept saying, 'Why won't you let me enjoy this?' and Marcos was trying to get him to understand this was nothing compared to what was about to be presented to him." The angel stopped and smiled. "You should have seen Abraham's face when he got to the Judgment Chamber. He was beaming from ear to ear. When he saw the Master, he ran right up to him and started hugging Him, too."

Winston seemed so at home here as the angels spoke about people coming and going. They shared about serving on earth and spending time in the third heaven of God. They laughed and took turns as they told their stories to Winston. People passing by looked at them hanging out together.

SUDDENLY

So be on your guard! Remember that for three years I never stopped warning each of you night and day with tears. Acts 20.31

"Winston, we have to go. Actually, you have to go. This has been straightened out, and you are here early. You will return to the entry area and disembark from this body." Marcos turned and politely offered to let Winston go first as they started back across the room. As they walked, Winston looked around. He could not have ever imagined the process needed to handle so many people over and over. Now he was aware of the truth. He had looked into the eyes of those who had drawn their last breath on earth and seen the overwhelming majority were not ready.

"What happened that I am going back?"

"After twenty minutes flatlined, they were able to revive you on the way back to the hospital."

"So, I get another go at life? After seeing all this, I will certainly want to make some changes. I will want to get some things worked out so when I come back. I am better prepared."

"Have you not been paying attention to what happens here. This all comes down to the person's name being in the book of life. That requires a personal commitment and surrender. You don't straighten this out yourself. In fact, you can't do it yourself. That is the whole point of Jesus' life and His death and His resurrection."

Winston was walking a little faster now and not

paying attention. He wanted to get back, being around so many dead people was not what he wanted to do. "So how does this work when we get back. How do I get my body back and what happens to this one?

"Keep walking toward the mist, and you will pass over, and you will wake up in your old body. Don't expect it to feel near as good as this one does. Especially after what just happened. Winston…"Marcos had stopped and waited for him to stop and turn back. "I don't know how long you have before you come back. It could be hours, days or years or it could be a few brief minutes. That does not matter. You need to make sure you are ready to come back here. I have the feeling that you are getting the opportunity most of the people here would do anything for. I would say give their souls for, but that is the whole point of passing through here."

Winston walked toward the mist. He stopped and looked back. A group of angels surrounded Marcos. Two red, one blue, one white and four who were various shades of peach or orange. Beyond them were the lines. Always moving and filled with people who only moments before were going about their lives as if they had plenty of time. He turned and started walking into the mist.

A Second Chance

Be very careful, then, how you live—not as unwise but as wise, making the most of every opportunity, because the days are evil. Therefore do not be foolish, but understand what the Lord's will is. Ephesians 5.15-17

Winston James Cummings doesn't know it, but he has just five minutes and thirty-four seconds to live as he opens his eyes. It has been eleven days since the accident. There are more pins in the bones of his body than has ever been used before on any other living single person. No one knows how he has survived the accident or lived this long. When the firefighters arrived, they worked on him for twenty minutes to bring him back to life. He was then transported to the regional emergency center where the worst accident victims are taken. Upon arrival, the emergency room doctors were so shocked by his condition; they were astonished that anyone was able to revive him. Internal organs were damaged, 90% of the bones in his body were broken or cracked from the force of the impact with the two vehicles and the street pavement. He had a series of surgeries to piece his body back together and was placed into a coma to deal with swelling of his brain. The doctors told his wife they see little hope of a full recovery and when he wakes it may be brief. She has not left his side and knows the full ramifications of what is about to happen.

The tube has been removed from his throat as the doctors begin to push the drug designed to wake him up through the IV in his chest. The damage to his arms is so extensive the circulation would not handle the IV. The room is quiet as the doctors and nurses work. As Winston starts to open his eyes the doctor signals for the nurses to step back and his wife moves close to his side. The heartbeat on the monitor shows the heart is beating at 165 beats per minute. It is fighting to keep the body alive. The blood pressure is not currently being read because there is no place to put the pressure cup to take a clear reading without causing further injury. Winston opened his eyes and looked around slowly. His wife smiled as she kissed his cheeks. His mind is racing, "Is this real, where am I, what has happened?" Sarah tries to calm him.

"Take it easy. You have been in an accident. You were dead for twenty minutes and were revived. The doctors have done everything they can." She stopped, a tear running down her cheek. "The whole church has been praying for you." She looked toward the door and then back to him. "Everyone has been such a help. Bridget, who used to work for you, has been staying with the kids and is bringing them in to see you. She has been such a blessing. As soon as she heard about the accident she came over and has been with us."

Every word was clear and distinct. Winston nodded his head. It hurt, it really hurt. It must be bad, but how bad could it be? He was not dead; he was alive. He could make things right with Sarah, the kids, at work, this was a second chance. Winston had less than five minutes to live.

"Winston, Pastor Bob is here. He wants a minute with you." She looked up to the other side of the bed. Winston turned his eyes and saw Pastor Bob bending down.

"Winston, I prayed that I would get at least thirty seconds with you. It is not good, and you need to be ready for what is about to happen. I want to ask you a simple question and offer you help." The pastor paused and looked for some affirmation Winston understood.

Winston shook his head no, "Not now pastor. I will deal with that later." His voice was raspy and cracked as he spoke. He had had a tube down his throat for eleven days. He wanted to wave the pastor away, but his arms would not move for him. He was confused about why his body was not working.

"Winston." It was his wife. She was whispering, and tears were running down her cheek. "I think you need to hear what the pastor has to say. The doctors don't think you have long."

He softly shook his head no again. At that moment he looked past the doctors and nurses in the room and saw Bridget standing in the doorway. Their eyes met for a brief moment. She was crying and turned away holding to the doorway.

The girls came into the room and around to the side of the bed where the pastor was standing. He stepped back and let them come closer. The clock was ticking, and Winston was not ready for his next appointment. The girls were crying and unable to talk. They stood there and looked at him. There were metal pins along with huge metal rings on both of his arms and legs. Several intravenous lines were attached to his chest. His face was bruised, his left eye was swollen shut, and his head had been shaved to allow for the surgery that had been done on him to fix the enormous fracture in his skull. This would be the last time they saw their father alive.

The doctor in charge motioned for the staff to step back.

"Winston." It was the pastor speaking. "Are you ready to come before God?" He was searching for the fewest words to say what needed to be said. He was well aware of how little time was left.

Winston turned his eyes to the pastor. He was surrounded by his wife, girls, and his girlfriend. He was embarrassed and did not want to deal with this in front of other people.

The pastor spoke softly and clearly, "Winston have you asked him to forgive you and to come into your life?"

He could not bring himself to do it. He shook his head "no" for the third time.

The monitors began to beep, and several alarms began to go off. The staff moved to turn them off and at the same time to stay out of the family's way.

"Oh, God no." It was Bridget who cried out and ran from the room.

Winston shut his eyes. He felt lightheaded. His wife signaled the pastor to take the girls out. Pastor Bob looked at Sarah and whispered: "I'm sorry."

The younger one turned and cried out, "Daddy." She started back, but the pastor stopped her. Pastor Bob got down and brought her close for a moment. He whispered to her. Then he stood up, and they left the room.

Winston opened his eyes, and there was his wife. She bent over and kissed his cheek. "I love you." She whispered in his ear. He closed his eyes and felt his mind drifting away.

Winston opened his eyes and looked around. He was trying to get his bearings. Everything felt different, almost dreamlike. Then he knew where he was, and he was not ready. He started walking in the darkness. He walked past people who were confused and those who were trying to push their personal walls back into the darkness. There was a man who was sitting on the ground crying. He did not care why. He was gathering his thoughts, and his fear was growing by the second. Had he really had a second chance? Then he heard the voice of Marcos. "Back so soon? Well, I hope you got things right. Very few ever get a second opportunity as you did."

Winston tried to speak, but the fear of what was coming had taken his voice. He started to step back but his invisible wall prevented any retreat. He knew this time being here was not some mistake. This time it was forever. He had missed his opportunity. Eternity had hung on five minutes and thirty-four seconds. Winston found himself walking in a line of people. Most of them had their heads down. It was unreal as he walked. There were things he had not noticed before as a visitor. He had not taken it seriously even when he was facing the possibility of eternal judgment. The people kept moving, but they had no choice. The personal wall that kept them from going back also slowly moved them forward. Those who stopped discovered that after a short period it would bump up against them and they had no choice but to move or be pushed forward. He stopped, and the wall came up against his back and moved him. The force of the wall was unstoppable.

As he slowly walked, this time in line with everyone else, the people looked very different. Most had a stunned look on their face. They were adjusting to where they were and what was happening. There was the occasional person who stepped to the side to allow others to pass. They would stand looking around until their wall nudged them forward again. Some were confused, trying to understand what had happened and what was happening without even thinking about what was coming next. One man came marching forward passing most in the line. His posture and cadence were distinctly military. He was marching forward to meet his maker. When two people caused him to stop, he merely came to a parade rest position and waited. Winston approached him.

"Do you know what is about to happen?"

"Yes." Came a firm and yet quiet reply.

"Are you ready?" Winston asked. Inside he did not want to be alone in the mounting fear he felt.

"Yes, I am ready. I discovered Him in a combat zone over thirty years ago. I thought I was going to die and I asked for help. I promised to serve Him for the rest of my life. I thought I might be giving him the last few moments. It seems he had other plans. I was rescued and served another ten years in the service. When I got back to base that day, I went and saw a chaplain. I asked him to show me the way. He did not know what I was talking about. He was a religious man, but he did not know God personally. I called my wife and told her I needed to find a man who knew God to show me the way to live the rest of my life. She said that could be taken care of. I just needed to come home. When I arrived home, she was there with two of her friends and their pastor. She that is her pastor showed me the way by taking me through the Roman road[58] of salvation, and I surrendered to Him that day and prayed the sinner's prayer and have served him every single day since. I made a promise, and I have kept it because of the promises he made to me including forgiving all my sins and providing eternal life."

"Is that why you are in such a hurry?'

"No, not really. In my heart, I will always be a military man. I am reporting for my next duty station, and I don't want to be late. Today is the day appointed for me to die and face the judgment and there is no point in putting off or dragging my feet. I remember when I went to jump school at Fort Bragg NC. The day I was to jump from the tower for the first time I was slow, and the drill master stepped out and called up to me. 'What's the holdup number 31? Our numbers were on the helmet, so he knew I was number 31. Then he yelled as loud as he could. You signed up for this so get your ass down here.' So, I jumped. Well, I signed up for this too, so I am getting my rear to the front of this line where it belongs." He smiled and at the same time the hold up in front of him cleared. He popped to attention, smiled even bigger than before. "Well, I'm off." He looked at Winston. "Hope you are ready."

A small girl walked by, just short of bursting into tears, passed by looking for her mother. An angel stepped up and lifted her so he could look into her little brown eyes. "Hey, little one, how would you like someone to help you the rest of the way?"

She nodded her head, and the angel brought her close as the little girl wrapped her arms around his neck.

"Are you a real angel?"

"Yes, I am, and today I am your angel." They moved on, and the little girl stopped crying.

"Wow, I wanted a puppy, but daddy said no. Does he know I have an angel?"

"No, I don't think so, and you don't get to keep me. I am on loan till you get to the front. OK?"

"Sure, OK." And they were gone.

All around were lines, they were full of people of all ages, colors, male and female. Standing in the lines of judgment and rewards all moving toward a final appointment with God.

He thought of the times he had made fun of the religious and those who spoke of eternity, how he thought them stupid or in some way deluded of common sense. He thought of the physical world as real and the spiritual as a mist within the minds of feeble, frail people seeking relief from life and their failures and weaknesses. Now he knew this was real and it would be real forever. The world he had left behind was a passing mist that dissolves in the light and warmth of eternity. Here it was dissolved with the coming of death, and this was the preparation for eternal day or night, eternal life or eternal punishment.

Suddenly the handful of sermons his wife had dragged him to and which he had daydreamed through were all important and the points scored by some player who was on his fantasy football team meant nothing. What was it the pastor had said at Easter that he thought so odd at the time? Oh, yes. As he closed the message, he had lifted his arm upward and cried out. "Behold, now is "THE ACCEPTABLE TIME," behold, now is "THE DAY OF SALVATION."[59] Lowering his arm he had taken a moment for it to soak in and then continued as he looked around the sanctuary of the church. "You are not promised another year let alone another day, and since some of you will not be back here next year, I urge you to make a commitment and call on His name today for forgiveness." At the time Winston had thought what a rude and weird thing to say to a group of people on Easter Sunday. He would not attend church for a year, not even Christmas and then he would show up next year and show him how wrong he was. Only, he was right, and Winston was the one who should have been paying attention. That was the last sermon he heard, and it had been prepared for him, and he had missed it.

Winston also noticed that no one was on their knees asking for forgiveness. It is as if they all knew the time had passed for that. Here and there were people like he had seen before. Those trying to bluff their way through. He now believed they knew, too, but were hoping their outward bluster would carry them through. Inside, their hearts were melting in terror, filled with pain and anguish at knowing what was coming.[60]

Occasionally the angels would step up and guide someone forward. Either they were causing a problem and were about to discover the truth of their judgment or they were being singled out for their life's work. One shy man was brought out right in front of Winston.

A blue angel with yellow tips on his wings gently touched him on the arm. "Pastor Smith, will you come with me please?"

The pastor seemed completely surprised and blurted out. "Why me, I have done nothing special."

The angel seemed surprised. "Pastor you served the Master for forty-five years in the same small church. They could have paid you more, but they refused, you never complained. You did everything to take care of the people and the building. You made hospital visits, home visits, Wednesday night prayer lessons, Sunday school, morning messages, weddings, and baptisms. You counseled their children, helped with their marriages, and buried saints and sinners with the same grace. You labored in that church, telling them about the Master, never thinking about yourself. Your son died suddenly, and you never blamed the Master. You taught 'Every day was a good day with God,' and you lived that out every day no matter what happened. You drove old cars and purchased your suits at the thrift store. They remodeled the building, and then they fired you because they wanted a young pastor to go with the upgraded building. They were ashamed of you and your old car and your worn suits. Your wife cried when they mistreated you. King David knew the truth when he asked, 'who can stretch out his hand against the LORD's anointed and be without guilt?'[61] Each of them will have to give an account on how they treated their pastor."

Pastor Smith interrupted the angel. "No, I don't want that. I should have taught them better."

"NO." The angel spoke without letting him continue. "You went to another larger church where you worked with the seniors and visited. You and your wife have served well, and now it is your time to discover all that has been prepared. Please, come with me." The angel stepped back and motioned with his hand for the pastor to step out. In a moment they were gone toward the front. Several people stepped out of line to watch, but the front was still too far away to see what was happening. Even then, all they could see were the large doors and those in front of them waiting to enter the Crown Court.

Winston was the only one in the lines who knew exactly everything that was about to happen because he had been here before and he knew he was not ready. It really was a long, long line and he knew there was a blank space where he should have put his name. He stopped looking around as he had before. He had no interest in learning anything else. He knew everything he needed to know. Winston James Cummings began to weep as he was nudged along by his own personal wall. He was a short distance away from the doors marked Omega and Alpha, where he would meet the Alpha and the Omega Himself and be judged. His physical life had ended, and he was not ready for what was coming next.

EPILOGUE
A PERSONAL CHOICE TO MAKE

*Therefore God exalted him to the highest place
and gave him the name that is above every name,
that at the name of Jesus every knee should bow,
in heaven and on earth and under the earth,
and every tongue confess that Jesus Christ is
Lord, to the glory of God the Father.*
Philippians 2.9-11

Everyone will one day pass from this life through death's experience into eternal life. There they will face either eternal rewards or eternal punishment. There are no second chances or do-overs. *"Each person is destined to die once and after that comes judgment."*[62] Judgment can either be a positive that a person has prepared for, or it will be a negative because of their choices in life. It will be either the receiving of rewards, or it is a place of separation from God for eternity. It is a choice we must make before we die. Each person must accept Jesus as their personal savior.

The truth is *"Everyone has sinned; we all fall short of God's glorious standard,"*[63] no matter what you have heard from the modern popular culture. Sin is real and is clearly defined by God in His word.[64]

Sin does not just hurt our relationship with God. It places our eternal souls in jeopardy. *"For the wages of sin is death, but the free gift of God is eternal life through Christ Jesus our Lord."*[65] Death is eternal separation from God. It is the red ribbon that leads away from God forever. The free gift means it does not cost us anything, but it does not mean we can continue to live

125

our lives as before.[66]

There is good news. *"God showed his great love for us by sending Christ to die for us while we were still sinners."*[67] God has provided a way out through Jesus who is Savior, Messiah, and Lord. The death of Jesus on the cross as payment for the sins of all but is only valid when applied to each individual life by the person.

"If you openly declare that Jesus is Lord and believe in your heart that God raised him from the dead, you will be saved. For it is by believing in your heart that you are made right with God, and it is by openly declaring your faith that you are saved."[68] The need to accept Him personally is vital to our eternal relationship with God. This is not something we do in secret or wait until later to take care of. The name of Jesus and the gift of Jesus' Salvation experience are vital to our eternal lives. The scriptures are clear that *"Everyone who calls on the name of the Lord will be saved."*[69] The choice is available to you. Those who accept it will begin a life with Jesus that will be a full and enjoyable experience.

Accepting Jesus' sacrifice for your sins and asking him into your life is where the Christian life and experience begins. It is part of His greater plan for our lives which is outlined in the book of Hebrews chapter 6 verses 1 & 2. *So, let us stop going over the basic teachings about Christ again and again. Let us go on instead and become mature in our understanding. Surely we don't need to start again with the fundamental importance of repenting from evil deeds and placing our faith in God. You don't need further instruction about baptisms, the laying on of hands, the resurrection of the dead, and eternal judgment.*

There are six simple steps in the Christian life.

1. First, the person must REPENT: This is the

acknowledging of our sinful life and accepting Jesus into our lives as our Savior. How we respond at the beginning determines how we finish. This is a change of direction of a person's life away from sin and toward making the daily choices approved by God. This life of right choices is called, 'righteousness.'

2. Second, we must start living a life of FAITH: This is learning to rely on Jesus and His Holy Spirit to guide our lives. Putting your confidence in God on a daily basis is key to a victorious Christian life. This is discovering the blessings of God in daily living.

3. Third, we need to be OBEDIENT through participation in WASHINGS or BAPTISMS: This includes taking part in personal water baptism after a person makes a decision for God. Discovering that you are not the final authority for your life and that the Word of God, the Bible, has clear directions we need to follow.

4. Fourth, discovering our ministry through the LAYING ON OF HANDS. Each individual who calls on Jesus will discover that God has a plan and ministry for their life. This is a key as we discover He is not only our Savior, but he is also Lord of our life.

5. Fifth, we need to be ready for the RESURRECTION of THE DEAD when we receive our eternal bodies. Everyone gets these new eternal bodies. Death is not an option, it does not have to be the end, but the beginning. It is vital each person is ready.

6. Sixth, we will stand or more correctly bow at

our ETERNAL JUDGMENT before Jesus where we will either receive eternal life and rewards or everlasting punishment and eternal separation from God. This is all dependent on our willingness to surrender to Him and have our names added to the Lamb's Book of Life.

It is vital that you accept Jesus as your personal Savior and be ready when your time comes to appear before God in the Crown Court before the great white throne of God's Judgment because there are no second chances.

The first step is to **repent** and ask God to forgive you and to come into your life. King David prayed such a prayer when he found he was outside of the will of God. It is located in Psalm 51. Here is David's 'sinner's prayer for forgiveness and acceptance.' David's prayer may represent your prayer and personal needs. As you do, underline the portions that represent your request to God.

The Sinner's Prayer by David, the servant of God

Have mercy on me, O God,
    because of your unfailing love.
Because of your great compassion,
    blot out the stain of my sins.
Wash me clean from my guilt.
    Purify me from my sin.
For I recognize my rebellion;
    it haunts me day and night.
Against you, and you alone, have I sinned;

I have done what is evil in your sight.
You will be proved right in what you say,
   and your judgment against me is just.

Purify me from my sins, and I will be clean; wash
me, and I will be whiter than snow.
Oh, give me back my joy again;
   you have broken me—
   now let me rejoice.
Don't keep looking at my sins.
   Remove the stain of my guilt.
Create in me a clean heart, O God.
   Renew a loyal spirit within me.
Do not banish me from your presence,
   and don't take your Holy Spirit from me.
Restore to me the joy of your salvation,
   and make me willing to obey you.
Then I will teach your ways to rebels,
   and they will return to you.

Unseal my lips, O Lord,
   that my mouth may praise you.
You do not desire a sacrifice, or I would offer one.
   You do not want a burnt offering.
The sacrifice you desire is a broken spirit.
   You will not reject a broken and repentant heart,
O God.[70] Amen

As you begin this journey my prayer is that you always keep your focus on where you will finally end up when this life is over. Today your personal prayer of repentance can put your name in the Lamb's Book of Life and begin a lifelong journey toward eternity with God.

If you have accepted Jesus as your personal savior may I recommend the next step to you? You should learn the basics of the Christian life. These are outlined in Hebrews 6.1-2. I mentioned them earlier in this book. I have written two books about these.

Elementary Christianity
What every believer needs to know
By Bob Highlands III

And

The Journey
The six basic truths that are the foundation of the Christian Faith
By Bob Highlands III

ABOUT THE AUTHOR

Bob Highlands III

is a born-again believer. (July 5, 1971)
Husband married to college sweetheart Patti (May 9, 1975)
Artist (Pencil, Pen & Ink, Watercolor)
Father of April, Aaron & Andrew)
Grandfather to Liam & Rhys
Student
(BA in Bible from MidAmerica Christian University)
(Master of Theological Studies from
Anderson University School of Theology)
Pastor (45 years and counting)
Who strives to make the Word of God understandable
and applicable to the lives of all.

<u>Author</u>
Last to Leave:
What the Bible really says about the end of time.

Elementary Christianity:
What every believer needs to know.

The Real Jesus (series Journals & Study Guides)
The Life and Teachings of the Son of God.

The Story Unfolds

Is This Heaven For Real

Removing the Mask

The Journey
The six basic truths of the Christian faith.

Bobhighlands.com for more information

It's A Long, Long Line

END NOTES

[1] C. S. Lewis, The Great Divorce, (New York, Harper Collins, 1946, renewed 1973)
[2] Kenny Parker & Reba Rambo "It's a Long, Long Line" from 1970 album The Real Thing, the Singing Rambos.
[3] 1 Corinthians 15.42-44
[4] Matthew 25.46 Jesus speaking about what will happen after a person dies.
[5] Revelation 6.9
[6] Ezekiel 18
[7] Matthew 10.33
[8] Hebrews 9.27
[9] Revelation 1.15
[10] Revelation 1. 12-16
[11] Philippians 2.10-11
[12] John 16.8-11
[13] Revelation 21.27
[14] John 16.9
[15] Matthew 25.21
[16] James 3.1
[17] 2 Peter 2.1
[18] John 5.24
[19] Matthew 13.40-42
[20] Hebrews 10.31
[21] Mark 13.32
[22] John 15.14
[23] Matthew 7.23
[24] Proverbs 29.23
[25] Matthew 7.20
[26] Romans 14.11, Isaiah 45.23
[27] Matthew 25.46
[28] Matthew 25.41 "Devil and his angels." The word angels here means messengers and is in reference to all followers and may include the Devil, Demons or evil spirits and all those who reject Jesus as their Lord.
[29] Matthew 13.47-50

---

[30] Mark 9.44, 46, 46
[31] Matthew 25.41
[32] Revelation 20.10
[33] John 8.44
[34] Romans 3.23
[35] Romans 1.20
[36] Romans 6.23
[37] Romans 5.8
[38] Romans 10.9-10
[39] Revelation 21.11-15
[40] Revelation 21.27
[41] Isaiah 13 & 14 covers this in great detail.
[42] Isaiah 14.19-20
[43] Isaiah 14.12
[44] Isaiah 14.21
[45] 2 Corinthians 12.2
[46] 2 Corinthians 12.3-4
[47] Isaiah 14
[48] Ezekiel 18.4
[49] Galatians 6.8
[50] Romans 1.20
[51] Matthew 25.41
[52] Luke 8.32-33
[53] Revelation 22.8-9
[54] Revelation 2.20
[55] Genesis 50.20 Joseph response to his brothers for all the evil they had done to him.
[56] Genesis 18
[57] Hebrews 11.10
[58] The Roman Road of salvation uses selected scriptures from the book of Romans to explain the way to find Jesus as your personal savior. It shows the clear reason why and the results of not responding to God. A version of this along with a sinner's prayer by King David are included in this book in the Epilogue.
[59] 2 Corinthians 6.2

[60] Isaiah 13.6-8

> Wail, for the day of the LORD is near!
> It will come as destruction from the Almighty.
> Therefore, all hands will fall limp,
> And every man's heart will melt.
> They will be terrified,
> Pains and anguish will take hold of them;
> They will writhe like a woman in labor,
> They will look at one another in astonishment,
> Their faces aflame.

[61] 1 Samuel 26.9

[62] Hebrews 9.27 NLT

[63] Romans 3.23 NLT

[64] Sins are clearly outlined and named in the New Testament. See 1 Corinthians 6.9-10; Galatians 5.19-21; Ephesians 5.5; Revelation 21.8, and just in case your personal sin is not on the list Paul says and THINGS LIKE THESE.

[65] Romans 6.23 NLT

[66] John 8.10 "From now on sin no more." A woman had been caught in adultery and brought to Jesus. This was a trap being set by the religious leaders. Jesus did not fall for it and ended up shaming and embarrassing them till they all left. There alone with the woman Jesus gave her clear directions for what he required next of her. She was guilty of the sin of adultery but now had the opportunity to repent and leave her sinful life. He did not overlook her sin instead he challenged her to "sin no more."

[67] Romans 5.8 NLT

[68] Romans 10.9-10 NLT

[69] Romans 10.13 NLT

[70] Psalm 51.1-4, 7-13, 15-17 NLT David's prayer contains portions particular to his sins and relationship with God. As you pray your sinner's prayer you can add your personal request and needs. David's have been edited out for this book to focus on your personal repentance. As you study the life of David you will discover how his personal request were a vital part of his repentance. Your personal call for forgiveness and help are a vital part of your new relationship with God.

And inasmuch as it is appointed for men to die once and after this comes judgment, so Christ also, having been offered once to bear the sins of many, will appear a second time for salvation without reference to sin, to those who eagerly await Him. Hebrews 9.27-28

Made in the USA
Columbia, SC
29 March 2019